About The Author

Chris grew up in Basingstoke, Hampshire, in the south of England but relocated to the warmer climes of South Devon after graduating from Staffordshire University in 2005. He claims to have never had the ambition to be a writer when growing up but the signs were always there as he mostly enjoyed any opportunity to put his creativity to the test, whether it be writing short stories in English class at school or trying to pen song lyrics when he started teaching himself to play the guitar.

It wasn't until 2013, after discovering James Herbert's *Others*, that Chris decided to put more ideas on the page, etching out the arc for three short stories which eventually would come together to form his debut novel *Acolyte*, first published in 2015.

Chris has also authored two children's picture books and during the pandemic of 2020, moved into the world of podcasting. His show *Dead Men Talk* is dedicated to his love of all things creative and listeners can hear him talk about all of the many inspirations behind his work so far.

Other books by CHRIS TETREAULT-BLAY

The Wildermoor Apocalypse
Acolyte
The Sowing Season
Of Gods & Insects

Trickerjack
A Necessary End

Children's books
It's A Long Way To The Moon
It's A Long Night For Santa

Acolyte

The Wildermoor Apocalypse: Book One

By
Chris Tetreault-Blay

ISBN: 978-1916196520

10 9 8 7 6 5

For Marie, Oscar and Lorelei.

My sun, moon and shining stars within a world that is just beginning.

Acolyte

/ˈakəlʌɪt/ *noun.* **1.** a person assisting a priest in a religious service or procession. **2.** an assistant or follower.

"Do not be bound together with unbelievers; for what partnership have righteousness and lawlessness, or what fellowship has light with darkness?"   **2 Corinthians 6:1**

Chapter One

August 23rd 2001

The rain had forced him inside sooner than he planned. He had been lingering outside for almost an hour now. To passers-by he feigned interest in everything around him; the flowers, the notices on the board outside advertising that week's coffee morning for the lonely and gossip-hungry, even the poster for the Carols by Candlelight service from the previous December, that would not be changed for another couple of months. In all honesty he could not face entering the building.

He was scared. It had gone too far this time and he had no idea who, if anyone, could help him. But he had to try. Father Michaels had told him to visit if he ever needed guidance.

He stood at the entrance to the church and tried to control his breathing. Its imposing structure appeared as a fortress beneath the ever-darkening clouds above. St. Jude's had stood at the heart of the centre of Wildermoor for over five hundred years with only minor repairs to the roof required in that time, along with the occasional window repair when a stray cricket ball found its way into the place of worship during a heated Sunday afternoon league game. The locals from the neighbouring village felt an unusual sense of pride for the building.

Although Father Michaels, and those before him, had always preached the sanctity and safety of the Lord's home, Colin Dexler still felt like he was being judged, even before he stepped foot into the small lobby at the other side of the heavy front doors.

As the rain became more intent on driving him inside, he entered, stopping short of the next set of doors that led into the main body of the church. He did not belong there. He knew that. It felt wrong.

The church was empty, heightening Colin's sense of abandonment. He had been parentless for much of his life and did everything he could to escape people. At last he had found a place possessing the right vibe to make him feel comfortable and welcome. He knew, however, that Father Michaels was there. It was 11:00am; he had not long finished his morning mass and would not leave for another hour or so.

It was a Thursday and the cleaners had been in early that morning. The place reeked of polish and fake fresh flower scent expelled from a can. Colin suddenly felt nauseous, but he knew it had nothing to do with the fragrance.

He hurried to the small booth and stepped behind the curtain, sitting on the small wooden bench within the confessional and trying to calm himself. He heard small, faint footsteps patter across the polished stone floor and held his breath. They grew nearer and then came the scrape of the curtain being pulled across from the neighbouring booth. With a slight exhalation from the effort, Father Michaels took his place.

"Welcome, my child," the priest said, "I only wish that the Lord could have sent us better weather this summer."

"Forgive me Father, but I have sinned." Colin spoke in a rush, taking Father Michaels by surprise. This man was troubled, he always had been, but even by his standards the urgency seemed uncharacteristic.

"Colin, I glad you came."

"It has been thirty-five days since my last confession," Colin continued ignoring the priest's pleasantries.

Father Michaels let out a short sigh. He knew that this would remain business-like, as it always did with Colin Dexler. Colin only visited the church in times of need and was otherwise a recluse. He obviously did not want to linger or be seen to be there.

"What has been your sin?" There was a pause as he listened to Colin's troubled breathing through the grated partition that stood between them.

"I don't know."

"If you do not know how you have sinned, how do you know you have?" Michaels spoke as sympathetically as he could, realising this was going to be waste of his time.

"Because He has returned to me, so I must have."

Father Michaels sighed again, this time out of frustration. Three confessions so far this year had revolved around a shadow-like figure that Colin Dexler claimed was haunting him, responsible for any un-Christian acts he carried out. A lost boy, who had been raised without guidance from his parents or the Lord, was Father Michael"s professional diagnosis. In an attempt to extend a helping hand, the priest had reached out but Colin had declined the invitation to become a more active part of the Church.

"He is only in your mind, Colin. We have been through this before. You have nothing to worry about. You are responsible for everything you do, or do not do, and you can make these choices for yourself. No-one else."

"But he wants me to do things, or he says I will die." His voice started to break and Father Michaels detected a faint sniff as Colin tried to stifle his tears.

"What kind of things?"

"Terrible things."

This is going nowhere, thought the priest. Sometimes he did begrudge having to be the pillar of this community, but forced the thought back down deep into his subconscious. He would have to meet Colin on his level.

"When does he want you to do these things Colin?"

"Tonight."

The priest remained silent for a few moments, pondering how best to handle yet another of Colin Dexler's paranoia episodes. But something wasn"t sitting right with Father Michaels on this occasion. Each time Colin had visited him before now he had been convinced that he was just a troubled man looking for somebody else to blame for his actions. Countless numbers of his kind had passed through the church doors in the years he resided over the Wildermoor parish. Amongst them a few had seen their lives put back on the right track and were now regular active members of Michaels' congregation. Some of them simply wanted to hear the word "forgiveness" so that they could continue with their otherwise sinful existence, but without the added weight of guilt bearing down on them. However, Colin Dexler had always been the black sheep of the bunch.

"Go home, Colin. You will see that there is nothing to be afraid of. It is your home; everything in there is yours and is familiar to you. There is nothing – or no-one – who is going to harm you there."

Another bout of sniffling came from the booth as Colin tried to regain his composure.

"You don't understand Father, there are people in my house. I don't want them there." His voice was trembling more so now. Father Michaels could hear him shivering.

"Tell them to leave," he advised. "You have every right to do that. It's your home and no-one else should be there if you don't want them to be." Father Michaels felt like a parent telling their child that there was nothing living in their closet or under their bed. Colin Dexler was a grown man but his mind had not matured over the years. He still possessed the same infantile fears he had carried throughout his life.

"I can't. If they leave the house, I will die."

This is hopeless, the priest thought. *We are getting nowhere fast.* The priest had expected the poor man to visit him again but Michaels had dreaded breaking the bad news.

"Colin, I'm glad you came today as I'm afraid I have something to tell you." There was no response from Colin's side of the confessional box but Michaels could see that his eyes had shifted to look at him directly through the partition.

"I am going away for a while." Before he could continue he was met with desperate pleas.

"No, No…" Colin shook his head frantically, the tears starting to stream as he lost the ability to hold them back.

"There will be a new priest standing in for me, from the city," Michaels soothed, "You can talk to him."

"No!" Colin yelled defiantly. "He won't understand! Not like you do. Please, Father, I need your help."

"You'll be fine Colin, really. You can survive without me. I'm not saying that I will never return, one day I will. I just don't know when." The priest carried on attempting to calm Colin down, knowing that it was against practice to leave his box during a confessional. He wanted to shake the man and tell him to get a grip.

Hearing Colin's cries brought forth a rising feeling of fear, apprehension and doom within Father Michaels. He was doing the right thing, getting away from here. He had not been feeling well in the last few weeks. Something was building – within him and across the village and it was about to snap. In that moment he realised the source of his tension was Colin Dexler. Something about him was making him fear for himself and it was getting stronger every moment.

"Please, Father. Stay. I will do anything. I can't talk to anyone about…Him…Not like I can with you."

"Colin please. You will be fine." Michaels was struggling to hold his nerve together. He wanted to tell Colin to man-up but most of all he wanted to be as far away from him as possible. His own hands were starting to shake uncontrollably.

Suddenly a clanging came from the other booth as Colin stormed out, clattering the curtain against its rails and knocking over a hymn book stand situated next to the box on his way out. By the time Father Michaels managed to exit his own side Colin was beyond the first set of doors and through into the small lobby.

"Colin! Wait! Just calm down, we can talk about this!" Guilt now joined the affray of emotions coursing through Father Michaels while his whole body began to tremble. The shadowy figure lingered in the lobby, Colin's features dulled out by the glare of the sun shining in through the doorway behind him. The drone of the words he shouted echoed through the empty walls of the church and remained with the priest for many weeks to come.

"Just don't blame me! I asked for your help, Father. Remember that!"

Before Michaels could take another step forward, Colin was gone.

Dexler dragged his slightly overweight form home in the only ungainly sprint that he could manage. Father Michaels remained still for a few moments, letting their exchange repeat over and over in his mind.

He had to leave and it had to be now.

He rushed to his vestry, removed his robes and hurriedly put them away in the small wooden wardrobe behind the door. He picked up the receiver of the telephone on his desk and dialled out. He stamped his foot impatiently, waiting for a voice to answer at the other end. At last it was answered with a stern greeting.

"I'm sorry. I know this is out of protocol, but we need to meet...No, you come and pick me up, it would be quicker…My things are here with me…No, no-one suspects anything. I have told them already that I am taking a sabbatical."

He looked at his watch in response to the directions given to him by the voice on the other end. "Very well, please hurry…Yes, call the others…I believe that the time is near."

Thirty minutes later, Father Michaels was standing anxiously by the back door to the church, which exited through his vestry. He held a suitcase in his hand. All his worldly possessions fit into the one case. Having lost all that meant more to him three years prior, when his wife of forty-six years was taken from him, nowadays he travelled light.

He stepped outside when he saw the black Mercedes pull up to the side gate at the far end of the cemetery. Hands still shaking – more so now – he locked the door and deposited the key beneath a plant pot on the third gravestone to the left of the gravel path. He transferred a kiss from his lips, with his hand, to the top of the headstone.

"Please forgive me," he asked of the slab, which bore the engraving *Anthea Michaels 1935 – 1999."*

His head was bowed as he walked away and got into the car. He did not look back as the car sped off before he had even been able to secure his safety belt.

Chapter Two

February 18th 1684

The night was cold outside. Franklin James felt the chill on his neck as if a thousand pins were stabbing him. When the breeze brushed against the sweat, he shuddered. But he was not outside. Franklin sat in his armchair, which was as weathered as the stone-walls of his humble cottage and as the old man himself. Even the embers from the flickering fire, flying up to touch his cheek with several warming kisses, could not stop the shivers.

The front door was no match for the chill either. For years it had been battered by bouts of harsh winter rain and wind from across the moors and failed to fight off the inevitable attacks from woodworm. It now clung to its hinges drunkenly, almost inviting passers-by to enter the house and help themselves. Not that Franklin had much of any value. Not anymore. He felt that the past few years had been sent to mock him, as the yield on his potato crops - for which he was known throughout Wildermoor - had dried up without warning. Franklin had to watch as his customers - and livelihood - walked away from him. He had lost his wife to the cholera epidemic that had gripped the villages two Christmases ago, leaving him to wither away. She had been the life and soul of him and had given him his most precious belonging – their daughter Evelyn.

But now she was gone too.

Franklin cursed himself for what must have been the hundredth time that night. The door creaked again against the strain of the relentless wind that seemed determined to break into the house. The creak did nothing more than to fan his guilt. When his business had dried up, he'd drunk away what was left of his profits. There was no more money left for the upkeep of what had been the James'' family home.

He had been meaning to fix the front door for the past eighteen months but had always found a reason not to. He blamed the door. It should have been secure enough to protect them, especially when they were vulnerable at nightfall.

Then he blamed himself. Again.

He had become weaker over the years, letting himself succumb to the damage brought on by years of toil, working the land to support his family. Arthritis had racked his hands and joints, grief and drink had weakened his heart. Now he was unable to protect his daughter when she needed him most. That night his legs had failed too. He had been awoken by her screams, which he heard as clear as a bell from his room at the back of the cottage. Only the open living area separating the bedrooms lay between them, with no walls to muffle the cries. For those moments, Evelyn was to Franklin but a baby again; defenceless, scared, and vulnerable. That sound lived with him with every minute, as would the time it had taken him to raise himself out of his bed and stagger down the short hallway which linked his wing of the home to hers.

He knew he was too late the moment he reached the central living room. Her screams had stopped. For a few fleeting seconds, he thought it was a dream he had finally managed to wake from. Then as he edged closer to the husk of the front door, which lay open to the elements, feeling the biting wind as it whistled into their home, his blood too ran cold. He could hear Evelyn's faint cries across the clearing of the fields, getting fainter with each turn of his head, desperately trying to locate her in the darkness. Once or twice, he thought he could hear her calling him, as if it was eighteen years ago and she was still lying on the sheepskin rug behind where he stood now in front of the flickering fire.

But Evelyn was gone. He knew it then, just as he realised there was no warmth from the fire. Franklin could even sense the presence of snowflakes starting to fall, the wind brushing them inside onto the cold stone floor in place of the sheepskin rug.

He sat staring into the flames that cast forth shadows of that night that was now four days in the past. Searches had been fruitless but persistent. For a while the local folk around him had admired Franklin for his success on the crop plantation he had acquired and grown to an enviable size. Now they pitied him as they watched him sink deeper into himself and become swallowed by his grief. They wanted to help though, even if it was to just give the old man a thread of hope to cling to. However, they too were beginning to flag with the effort of the long days and nights they committed to the cause, knowing that with each day they were getting closer to having to call off the search.

Franklin decided to pour himself another drink – a brandy. It seemed that this was the only comfort and warmth he could afford himself. It also helped mask the images in his head of where Evelyn might be, of what might be being done to her, or even whether she was alive. But it only numbed the pain for a few seconds. He took another gulp from the tankard and waited as he felt the alcohol warm his throat, continuing down through his body, hazing his mind. It had become almost like his best friend over the last couple of years, always there when he needed to forget.

Franklin heard the door creak open again. It felt different this time. The bitter chill did not come with the sound but he could sense a presence. Edward Childs, Franklin's oldest friend, former business partner and the current landlord of The

Weary Traveller stood in the doorway. Franklin turned his head to greet him from his chair.

Edward showed signs of wear and tear himself. His hands were rough and knotted from years of manual labour on the moorlands that had afforded him the chance to settle into retirement, the revenue from the Traveller helping to keep money trickling in. Edward too had experienced loss over the years, but he emitted a strength and reserve that Franklin did not, and had undertaken the role as chief of Evelyn's search party. Edward stood in his thick sheepskin coat and heavy boots, his shoulders lightly dusted from the beginning of another snow shower. His eyes were rimmed with black, heavy bags underneath highlighting the lack of rest from the last few nights.

Franklin raised his eyebrows as a greeting but Edward returned it with a solemn shake of his head. This had become a silent code between the two at the end of each day. Franklin clung on to the hope that Edward would finally offer him a nod.

Edward removed his boots and brushed off his coat and laid them down on a stool at the side of the door. He sat in the other armchair opposite Franklin. The chair had previously belonged to Christina-Rose, Evelyn's mother. She and Franklin had spent many an evening sitting opposite each other, looking into each other's eyes as the night drew in. Franklin couldn't seem to pull himself away from this tradition, even now, and his eyes always showed a hint of disappointment when their gaze met Edward's.

Edward broke the silence.

"The frost has already started to set in across much of the ground."

Franklin nodded slowly in reply, his eyes fixed on the cold floor. It was debatable whether he even listened to anybody when they spoke these days.

"There's more in the air, and the snow is beginning to fall," continued Edward, "It is going to make it hard for us to find any tracks come dawn." This time there was no response, not even a cursory nod from Franklin.

"Frank, you must really start to consider-"

"No." Franklin snapped. "Just don't."

Edward sat in wait, considering the best choice of words.

"It's been four days, that's all."

"Then we are one day closer. She is still out there, Ed."

Edward, feeling that this was not a conversation that was best pressed at the current time, stood up, gave Franklin a loving pat on the shoulder and nodded. He then walked over to the canteen on the sideboard, popped the stopper on the crystal decanter and poured himself a swig of brandy. He downed the measure in one, exhaling sharply as it stung his throat. He was not as accustomed to the taste as Franklin. After another hard day in the scathing wind, scouring every inch of the plantation and surrounding woodland, he needed it to soften the edges. Edward placed the glass on the sideboard once more and poured himself another.

"I can't give up on her. You know I can't," Franklin said behind him. "I made a promise," he referred to the dying wish he had granted his beloved Christina, that he would always protect their daughter.

"I know you can't, and none of us are going to. I loved-" Ed started, before catching and correcting himself, "I still love her like she is my own daughter, Frank."

Franklin gave a knowing nod and felt the tears sting as they welled up again. He brought his hand up to his mouth to stifle his cry. His unkempt stubble scratched against his fingers, reminding him how little he had managed to look after himself. Edward could see for himself that Franklin was a shell of the strong figure he used to be and felt a sadness overcome him. He had once been a pillar of the community. Now it seemed he was merely clinging to existence.

The two friends sat mostly in silence well into the night, fighting sleep in front of the radiating warmth. Franklin hadn't slept in days – not well, anyway. Edward assumed the role of his protector too, and gave him the security he needed, if only brief, so that Franklin could let his body submit to the darkness for a little while. He slept now, as Edward gently reached over and removed the tankard from the old man's hand. It had served its purpose well once again. This was another of the rituals Edward had become accustomed over the last few days. Then Edward sat back into his chair and closed his eyes.

Chapter Three

Franklin reached the doorway and wearily clung to the dilapidated frame to steady himself. He dared not look outside from fear. Edward stepped into the snow without his sheepskin coat and sheepskin lined boots. The rider halted the horse in the courtyard at the front of the house. It was then that Franklin's heart sank back into its cave. The voice that greeted them was not that of his daughter.

The rider climbed down off of the horse and Edward embraced him immediately, with each giving the other hard pats on the back like long-lost brothers. It was not Evelyn. It was Ewan, Edward's middle son. With his arrival came more apprehension for Franklin. Edward had appointed Ewan his main foot soldier in the search for Evelyn. He would not have come back from his post without good reason… or harnessing bad news.

Edward hugged his son close as if it had been years since they last met.

"I was certain I had sent you to your death in this storm," Edward said, the relief blossoming with his words. Then once again aware that it was not the right time to show this emotion for his son's return, he released Ewan from his grip. The young man's eyes then met the gaze of the pleading old man in the doorway.

Franklin stood with expectation written over his face, his eyes searching Ewan's for any hint of hope he could muster.

Ewan took a sharp breath in preparation for the inevitable questioning. He had ridden for so many miles, playing this moment over and over in his mind. Not once had he convinced himself it was going to be easy.

"Please don't make me ask. Save me from any more uncertainty," Franklin pleaded.

Ewan's gaze stayed strong. He did not want to betray Franklin's trust nor dash his hopes with a harsh truth.

"We have found a trail," he said finally, "something which we believe can lead us to her."

Franklin could hardly feel the air in his lungs and his heart pounded in his ears as the blood rushed trying to keep him from passing out in the cold.

"We found this." Ewan handed over a silver locket on a slender chain that had been broken in two. Franklin's hands trembled as he took hold of the locket. He clenched his fist around it with the little strength he could muster. He knew it well. It was the gift he had given to Evelyn on her sixteenth birthday; the day after her mother had died. He dared not open it but needed to know for certain.

Finally Franklin prised it open. There staring back at him were those enchanting eyes and sultry black hair tied up on the back of the woman's head and cascading down to the nape of her neck. The image of Christina-Rose never ceased to bring a chill to his bones as well as warming his very soul. A tear welled in his eye as memories and fears came flooding back in a torrent.

"Where?" Franklin asked struggling to make his voice resonate.

"About twenty miles west. There's a track through the woodland leading to Harper Falls," Ewan seceded. "We were more than fortunate to have found anything before the snow set in."

"We must go," Franklin offered immediately.

"Not tonight." Knowing his old friend would not listen, Edward spoke with authority. "We all must rest before making such a trek. You have barely slept and are not strong enough to stand more than a few minutes in these conditions."

"No, we have wasted too much time already," Franklin shot back. "I have been kept here for so long just waiting for one of you to come back to tell me the worst and now you are telling me not to go?"

"My father is right, Mr. James," Ewan interjected. "A few more hours will not hinder our search. The track will already be covered by snow. We will need the morning sun to chase it away so that we do not die in the cold trying to retrace my steps. We can set off at dawn."

"Then dawn it is," Franklin relented, "But no later. And don't expect me to sleep."

Chapter Four

February 18th 2002

The rattle and splutter of the coffee machine did little to please Dr. Lorraine Thacker. The pathetic drip-drip of the black liquid into her Brookdale University mug do nothing but test her patience. It had been a long, late night and she was in no mood to be tested by the office equipment. Patience was the one thing that she could not afford to leave the house without, since this was the one quality she needed to offer to her other kind of patients; the ones that paid her what many of them probably felt was an extortionate amount of money for an hour of her time. In this case it was the ones that Wildermoor Brook Psychiatric Unit could not deal with or figure out on their shoe-string budget so passed on to her.

With a final gasp and strain, the last of her coffee filtered through to its receptacle and Dr. Thacker retrieved the mug and took her first gulp. It burned her throat but warmed her senses and relaxed her a little, enough to provide the current patient with her undivided attention.

Colin Dexler had been a particularly complex case. Forty-three years old, no job, no family of any recent record. Found one night, locked in his one-bedroom dwelling in the centre of Wildermoor town, screaming maniacally about a phantom, his hands covered in blood that traced from where he stood in the lounge back through to the kitchen, smeared across the floor and walls and ending at the kitchen sink.

Within minutes Dexler was face down on his tattered and stained shag-pile carpet as his hands were manacled behind his back and he was hauled away. Despite three intensive days searching, the police could find nothing. No weapon. No body. No victim. No missing persons reported. No motive. No case. So Dexler was freed but ordered to live his days under psychiatric observation.

That was when Dr. Thacker had been introduced to him. Wildermoor Brook was deemed to not have the manpower to commit itself to the care of Colin Dexler, which was another way of saying that they wanted no part of his case. Henceforth there would be no blood on their hands if they could not control him or cure him. Nobody wanted to shoulder that responsibility.

Dexler had been put into Dr. Thacker''s care five months previous. There had been very little in the way of recent criminal activity on his part but his ramblings were causing concern for the medical staff and law enforcers alike; concerns for *his* safety and ultimately, their own. Lorraine had been tasked with trying to crack the origins of his paranoia. Some had suggested trying to lure him into committing a violent or abusive act so that they would have enough evidence to elevate his case to the point where he could be incarcerated.

Lorraine had been horrified by this suggestion, for fear of putting herself in danger and also because she believed that Colin Dexler was not the monster others perceived him as. He was scared, she could see that. She believed the act of possessing a fear should not be exploited or manipulated. Colin had started to open up lately and she believed that whichever Colin Dexler the police had found that night, was not the one who sat before her today.

Colin sat on the edge of the padded chair, his feet crossed, hanging down and both hands clasped together, his arms hanging limp into his lap. He had lost weight in recent weeks; she could tell. His eyes looked to be receding into his skull and his skin appeared to be hanging from his face. She had never seen him smile and wondered how dramatically his appearance would be alter if he simply raised the corners of his mouth. The hair on his head was closer-cut than before, and greying.

Lorraine grasped her coffee mug as she turned and walked back to her chair opposite the one in which Colin slumped. She looked at him with pity. He reminded her of a wounded pet that she felt unable to offer help.

"I would offer you some coffee," she offered, "but I believe the caffeine would interfere with your medication."

Since his arrest Colin had been on a course of antipsychotics. Colin looked up to meet Dr Thacker's face, his eyes drooping at the sides before sinking once more towards the floor.

"How do you feel today?"

Colin shrugged his shoulders and mumbled something which Lorraine couldn't decipher. "Are you sleeping well?"

"Sleep?" Colin replied surprising himself as much as he did the doctor. His voice was slow and his speech slurred. "No." He concluded.

"You're having problems sleeping?"

"It never comes."

"Why is that?"

"He tells me that I can't sleep. I'm not allowed to."

"Who's He?" Lorraine prompted knowing that she was making ground as she had done in the early stages of their first meetings. She also knew who He was but it was a sure-fire way of enticing Colin to talk. He was like a clam that would only open with encouragement. Once he left her office the shell locked tight again and the cycle would repeat in a week"s time. She had been trying to secure a daily or even bi-weekly programme for Colin. She believed it vital to his treatment that he not be given a chance to descend back into himself.

"You know," he replied curtly. Colin did not like to be asked to repeat himself nor did he enjoy having to discuss the horrors that visited him every night.

"I want you to tell me."

"No."

Lorraine could see Colin was beginning to become agitated at the questioning. She wasn't sure if he even remembered what they discussed in their previous sessions from one week to the next, but she knew it was definitely a sensitive area.

"Are you afraid, Colin?"

He looked at Lorraine, his eyes parting wider to reveal the bloodshot whites, showing how little rest he receiving. *The medication cannot be working*, she thought. The man is constantly on edge and is at risk of a heart attack or stroke if he does not calm down. He looked frail as he stared at her, as if he might crumble to ashes at any moment.

Colin was looking past Lorraine, over her right shoulder, staring into the far corner of the room. Lorraine felt eyes boring into the back of her head; she was being watched. She turned her head over her left shoulder but saw nothing but the empty space between the two tall grey filing cabinets in the corner of her office.

Apprehensive but now convinced that nothing was lurking behind her, she turned back to Colin, but jumped with a start to find that he was now sat mere inches from her, on the pine coffee table. His eyes were drawn wide into an unnerving stare as if they were drilling a hole through into her head.

She felt a warmth surge through her, up from her legs to her fingertips, travelling up her arms until she could feel burning in her head behind her eyes. Colin stared still, without as much as a sound that would suggest he was breathing. Not moving his eyes, he spoke once more.

"I shouldn't be here. He says I shouldn't be here," he uttered slowly, calmly.

Feeling her breath catch in her throat she asked again. "Who?"

The question seemed to bounce off of him like a rubber bullet. Colin did not appear to acknowledge that Lorraine had spoken. She was scared now too; his eyes were wild and his body rigid, a coiled cobra ready to strike. Lorraine instinctively reached out her hand to try and calm him. She had worried about him these last few weeks and went into every meeting not knowing if he would make it through the following days alive. Now he was scaring her to the point where she could not breathe. The warmth in her head was becoming unbearable and beads of sweat now formed on her brow. Was she now the one at risk of her body shutting down from fear?

Lorraine's hand carried on reaching for Colin resting on his left shoulder. As soon as she touched him his eyes came back to life as if she had flicked an invisible switch. Colin shook his head twice as if awakening from a dream and looked around the room frantically trying to regain his bearings. He started to pant and whimper, his eyes glistening as the tears formed.

Lorraine had suffered another start herself when the mannequin figure before her came back to life. She placed her hand once more on Colin's shoulder, with more force this time, in an attempt to comfort him.

"Shhh-shhh, it's okay, Colin," she said calmly, "It"s only me." But it was no use. His breathing was out of control and his head was thrashing from side to side with such force she worried his neck would snap. His eyes were clenched shut as he started to sob.

"Colin, it's Dr. Thacker, you're in my surgery and you are safe…" she pleaded with the authority of a pre-school teacher trying to calm a distressed boy.

"Just go away," he pleaded, "Leave me alone. What do you want from me?" His voice started to break into a scream as he struggled for breath through the tears. "WHAT DO YOU WANT FROM ME?!"

Dr. Thacker started to shake him gently to snap him from his trance and within seconds the light faded as Colin opened his eyes. He looked around the room once more but it had changed. He was no longer sitting or standing. His duvet cover lay crumpled on the floor and his bed sheets were torn from the mattress at one end. The light was straining in through a crack between his bedroom curtains. He did not want to face the light of another day but was terrified of spending another second in the darkness.

Dr. Thacker had brought The Reaper back to him. And now, in order to save himself, she had to go.

Chapter Five

As Thomas Laing unlocked his car, he knew he would regret opting to spend yet another lunchtime in what had become a portable diner over the last few weeks. As he opened the door to his trusty 1992 Vauxhall Astra, the warm, stale air rushed out and embraced him. As tradition required, Laing quickly grasped the handles on the inside of the doors and wound the windows down. A year of police training meant that he could not afford himself a new steed, with automatic windows and decent seals to prevent the damp or air conditioning. This new-fangled technology was beyond his reach for now, but he vowed that he would press on and ruthlessly clamber to the top of the ladder, or even a few rungs from the bottom in order to kit himself out with these luxuries.

For now, Laing had to make do with a driver's seat as comfortable as a mattress stuffed with bricks, and having to sit for half of his lunch break with the door open to let the stubborn and rank air escape the car, allowing any passers-by of Exeter Street a glimpse into his lunchbox. Every day this consisted of the same contents: a flat peanut butter sandwich, a somehow-melted chocolate biscuit and a packet of DIY Ready Salted crisps (the ones that came with salt in a blue wrapper and required you to shake salt onto the crisps yourself, then to realise that the salt was laying at the bottom of the bag having only tickled a few of the crushed crisp particles.)

Today held no promise of being any different than the other ten that Laing had spent with the Wildermoor Criminal Investigation Department so far. In essence, he was a tarted-up tea boy and data-inputter. Sure, Chief Detective Inspector Darke was a great mentor, but he had a reputation of putting all of the new pups through every menial task imaginable before they were let loose and able to shadow one of the other more experienced officers on the day job. Laing knew that was where the real action was.

For days so far he had sat and listened in awe at them all coming back into the stuffy office on Percy Street, regaling tales of their travels. They were far from beat-bobbies; this was CID and they were the big boys called in to provide the muscle and the brains after the blues had laid the groundwork. It promised to live up to all of Laing's expectations, but he knew that patience was a virtue he must embrace if he was to succeed and join the elite. For now he just needed to remember who took milk and two sugars.

Laing unpeeled his sandwich from its film wrapping and gobbled it down. Breakfast was also not a luxury he afforded himself since his love of sleep and 6-am starts did not see eye-to-eye. Lunch would serve as his first and most hearty of meals. Once his hunger was satisfied Laing sat back in his driver's seat, his knees just brushing the sides of the steering wheel in an attempt to get comfortable. He glanced at his watch. It was 12:07pm. His lunch had successfully lasted four minutes. Now he had forty-nine minutes to himself to satisfy his need for sleep.

The rising mid-day warmth meant that Laing's eyes already sat heavy and catching forty winks would not be a problem. He pulled his door shut and manually locked it from within. As ropey and rusty as it was, he cherished this car. It had been his father's and held many fond memories. He couldn't stand to see his Dad sell it for a mere few hundred quid, so had given him the last of his savings the previous summer and bought it from him

Laing let his head fall back against the headrest and sleep soon came. He dozed on every lunch break believing it prepared him for the final push at the end of the day and would prepare him for the moment that DI Darke decided to throw him in at the deep end, which would only happen if an officer was unwittingly taken out of action and Laing found himself at the front-end of a drugs raid or bank-hostage situation.

Visions of grandeur danced before his eyes and within seconds he was asleep.

Chapter Six

Colin sat on the edge of his bed staring at the chunky gold-trimmed clock on his wall. The time was 11:10am and he still sat shrouded in darkness. He could not bring himself to open the curtains and welcome in another day, knowing what the day would likely bring him. Since his visits to Dr. Thacker had been increased to twice-weekly he had seen The Reaper every day without fail, sometimes even several times an hour.

*****

The first time the huge shadowy figure had visited him was when he was just seven years old. By then he had volunteered himself as a prisoner in his bedroom away from his parents. This was because he had born witness to some form of abuse from his father to his mother, ranging from verbal berating to holding a kitchen knife to her throat. On other occasions, he had suffered his father's wrath himself, as the welts and bruises across his back and legs proved. Careful not incriminate himself, his father had never struck him in the face.

The only way Colin had seen to avoid this was to stay away from his parents altogether and only report to the lower floor of the house to pick up his meals or to leave through the back yard on his way to school. In the end, he didn''t leave the house for weeks and his schooling was terminated at the age of nine.

One night he had been woken up by the sounds of screaming and slamming that he had become used to. He had wondered in what position his father had his mother pinned this time. He had seen it all and nothing surprised him anymore. Emotion had become a distant memory for Colin as he had trained himself to be soulless. Emotion led to caring and when you care about someone or something it could hurt. Ignorance and avoidance had been the only answer. On the night in question, the screaming had not seemed as if it would cease so Colin had pulled his head to his chest and clamped his eyes shut as hard as he could.

That had been when the smell came. And then the searing heat. It had all happened at once and so seamlessly that he had failed to acknowledge it as real. The room had filled with an odour that stuck in the back of his throat tickling his tonsils, making him want to gag. The smell of burning flesh had met with suffocating warmth that had appeared to be radiating around Colin's bed.

Colin had fought to close his eyes and make the smell and heat disappear but it had only grown stronger until he felt as though he was choking, gagging, unable to breathe. Colin had thrown back the covers but could see no flames or burning bodies. His room was as it always had been.

But as he had shifted his body over to lie on his left side, his comfortable side, he had seen Him. Or It. The figure had towered almost to the ceiling and stood what seemed at the time to be ten feet wide. It had arms; it vaguely resembled human. But it was shrouded in black from head-to-toe, a heavy hood pulled up over its head and a void so dark at the front that he could not make out a face. The putrid smell of burning flesh had returned slowly until it overcame Colin to the point he had lurched to the opposite side of his bed, thrown his head down and promptly brought up what little he had eaten.

As he had turned back trembling, towards the figure - his throat now burning - two shrivelled, red shapes had appeared at the ends of the arms of the cloak. Hands. The skin had appeared red raw, blistered and cracked with heat. They had been bleeding but the figure had moved the fingers as freely as Colin could his own, clenching and unclenching his fists in a display of perfect dexterity.

The moment It had lifted its head enough for Colin to make out two red orbs within the void of its hood, he had once again felt as though he was surrounded by flames. The figure had not moved but hung in the corner of the room. Colin's internal flight response had kicked in, moving his legs underneath him whilst his mind was still locked as one with the shadowy figure. When he had finally come to, he had been surrounded by total darkness once more. A wall of fabric had surrounded him, swaying as he turned his body left and right. There hung coats and shirts. One garment had seemed to hang the height of the room; his towelling dressing gown that his mother had forced upon him two Christmases ago. He was inside his wardrobe.

When Colin had finally summoned the courage and the involuntary trembling of his hands had slowed enough to push open the wardrobe door, his room was empty. He turned full circle to ensure he took in every corner of the room until he had been satisfied that the shadow was no longer there. He then sank down onto the floor and crossed his legs, gently rocking back and forth, regulating his breathing once more. Then the tears came, turning quickly into sobs. No-one had come to check he was okay. That had been the last time the Colin Dexler cried.

*****

Colin glanced once more at the clock on the wall, mocking him with its sarcastic ticks, drawing out each second as his next appointment with Dr. Thacker drew nearer. His hands began to tremble involuntarily, but he fought each with the other trying to hold them down and bury his palms in his lap. It was no use. The spasms were now spreading up his arms to his shoulders. His breath became shallow and coloured spots started to dance before his eyes.

Then he felt the room grow warmer. As his breathing lightened even more he could feel the first of the beads of sweat coat his neck. Then that smell. Overcooked meat slowly becoming stronger, the crackling sound of fat burning built in the distance.

His body bolted upright and ran for his bedroom door. Once Colin was through and into the darkness and cool of the small landing he slammed the door behind him. He rushed down the steep staircase that brought him to the long entrance hallway. He paused by the small telephone table halfway down and the handset started to chirrup as it rang. He cautiously lifted the phone but said nothing. After a pause, a tinny voice on the other end of the line greeted him,

"Mr Dexler? Hello?" Colin tried to speak but his throat was as dry as the desert and he could only muster a whisper.

"Hello?" The voice searched for Colin once more.

Colin tried again to force a sound but all he could muster was a dry wheezing.

"Is anyone there? Are you okay?" the voice asked, sounding mildly concerned but also irritated. The voice on the other end wheezed also and rasped as it spoke.

"We know you"re there, Colin. You can't hide from me. I'm everywhere."

Colin's breathing once more slowed and almost halted. His hands once more started to tremble from the sound of the voice he had come to fear for many years. As he started to whimper helplessly into the mouthpiece, he summoned the courage and strength to address the caller.

"Just leave me alone! What do you want from me? Just go away!" He slammed the receiver down and sobbing uncontrollably, ran for the front door. He could not display any weakness.

Once outside, he hung a right and ran to the narrow alleyway separating his house from his only neighbour. At the end of the passage, a rotten wooden door hung on its hinges that almost dropped to the ground every time Colin attempted to open it. He caught it this time expectantly and roughly threw it against the wall of the neighbouring property as it softly flopped to the damp ground with no more than a wet thump.

Dexler reached inside under a tower of brittle and broken plastic boxes and pulled out a small rusted toolbox. He clambered with the folding lid, which screeched as it opened, stiff and rusted from years of being left out in the winter cold and summer rains. Colin knew exactly where to find it.

He pulled out a twelve-inch long wrench, the only item that held a happy memory for him. He looked at the tool and fondled it before stashing it down through his right trouser leg and tightened his worn leather belt to hold it in place. He didn't bother to replace the toolbox or reposition the shed door to its rightful place. Colin turned and briskly walked back up the passageway and down the length of Exeter Street, not lifting his head to acknowledge any passers-by. Ten minutes was all it would take him to reach Wildermoor Psychiatric Institute.

Chapter Seven

The sound of the coffee machine often pleased Dr. Lorraine Thacker, but not today.

Her 11:00am appointment had not shown up. This would not have bothered her so much if it had not have been Colin Dexler who already took up time on most of her surgery days but had never missed or even been late to a session in the last six months. Of all of her patients, Dexler concerned her the most.

Lorraine placed her still-too-hot coffee mug on her desk and sat back down, immersing herself once more in Dexler's case file. Dexler's social history told of an abusive childhood and a broken home. He sought solace within himself, had no friends or known family. She felt that she had begun to make real progress with him up until a few weeks ago. Colin had almost cracked a smile and showed signs of relaxation. Then that all changed and it was as if the clock had turned back months. He would hardly engage in their sessions and spent most of his time looking at the floor. He feared meeting people's eyes.

A light tap at the door roused Lorraine from her notes. A head appeared from around the door as it opened and April, the surgery's receptionist, greeted her with a quick smile, which promptly fell back down from her face.

Lorraine spoke first.

"Any joy?" April shook her head regrettably.

"No, I'm afraid not, Doc. We tried calling several times. Eventually he answered but it was quite concerning…" Her voice trailed off, the last word hanging in the air between them.

"Concerning?" Lorraine asked showing concern of her own. "How do you mean? Did he speak?"

"Yes and no. All I could make out was that he wanted to be left alone, but he sounded panicked."

He wasn't the only one.

"I'd better visit and see that he's okay-" Lorraine said as she got up from her desk, grabbed her bag and headed towards the door.

April stepped from behind the door and motioned Lorraine to slow down.

"Don't rush out. I'm sure he is fine. He may even be on his way. He didn't say that he *wasn't* coming in today."

"Yes, but you also said you couldn't understand anything he did say," Dr Thacker fired back. "How do you know that he is okay?"

"I'm just hoping I suppose. For his sake. Listen, you can't rush out anyway as you still have your twelve o'clock. Duty of care, remember?" April reminded her, "Other people are depending on you too today."

Lorraine nodded and reluctantly hung her handbag onto the back of her recliner chair and popped herself back behind her desk. April said she would return with more coffee from the machine and gently closed the door. Now alone once more with her thoughts she started to imagine a host of horrid things that could be happening to, or at the hands of, Colin Dexler. The man clearly wasn't well and she was not doing her best to rehabilitate him. But for now she remained a prisoner behind her desk.

Deciding she needed to act, unable to settle properly until she knew Colin was not lying dead on his kitchen floor, she picked up the phone on her desk and spun the dial around to the one number she knew she could count on.

"Wildermoor Police.   Reception, Switchboard or Emergency?" the voice asked.

"Chief Detective Inspector Darke please."

"Certainly. Good morning, Lorraine," the voice greeted cheerily. "I will pass you through."

At the initial sound of his gruff, harsh, yet warming voice Lorraine instantly felt better, as she always did when talking to Truman Darke. They had a past, and had been lovers until six months earlier. Her old feelings had never truly died.

She hoped that perhaps he felt it too. Truman had been the only man who had made her feel secure even since their affair had ended. As a result, this was the first time she had felt comfortable being alone.

Once the usual niceties were out of the way, Lorraine heard his tone change when she revealed the real reason she had called him. Truman made no attempt to stifle his frustration at her request.

"Truman, I know you don't like the guy."

"Not *like* him?" Truman roared startling Lorraine. "That's putting it a little lightly. The man has single-handedly stunted my career and is a monster to boot."

"I know how you feel, Truman and I hate asking you but I really am worried. He has not missed a session in six months. I believe I might be on the verge of a breakthrough with him but there is also a chance he is on the brink of destroying himself."

Truman resisted the urge to add *good riddance* to her last remark knowing it would neither help his cause nor change her mind. In his eyes, Lorraine had developed an unhealthy interest in the Dexler case. He hated that she had been offered the assignment in the first place, let alone that she willingly accepted. He had tried to open her eyes to the danger surrounding this but she would not quit.

"You know I wouldn't ask you if I didn't need your help," she continued, assuming his brief silence was softening the armour he wore when it came to Dexler.

Truman had been on the brink of being made Commissioner when he was handed the homicide investigation concerning one Colin Dexler. This was a sure-fire hit, he was told. All he had to do was prove that the man had murdered three people in the most brutal manner, and the promotion - not to mention the entire Wildermoor Police Department - would be his.

The crime scene itself would have made the most hardened horror film fanatic and those who write of societies" sinister side question how far their imagination could carry them. Truman had not slept for days, even weeks, after visiting the scene. The smell from the blood-soaked carpet, walls, sofas, stairs and bedsheets, remained with him, especially when he closed his eyes at night.

The filthy house had been searched thoroughly from top to bottom, the floors taken up, the garden dug up and no sign of the bodies had been found. But the smell of cooked, boiled and burnt flesh lingered in the walls of that house. Everything pointed to Dexler having committed the most atrocious act of torture and murder. They had found him locked in a first-floor bedroom with a bloodied meat cleaver — an obvious murder tool - lying in the far corner away from him. The suspicion was that he had cooked and eaten the bodies, disposing of the bones who-knew-where.

As far as the powers-that-be were concerned, Truman had no case. It had been thrown out by the judge due to a lack of evidence. Despite Truman's request for an extension to the case, so that he could delve deeper and put Dexler through intense psychological and psychiatric assessment, the judge had denied him.

Instead they released Dexler from the safety of his cell and back into the wild, with a flimsy programme of cognitive assessment the only form of justice. Taking nothing away from Lorraine Thacker's ability, Truman saw this as child-minding a man he believed was a proven killer. The decision to explore the man's mind was merely the result of his incessant ravings that a phantom was controlling him.

"What do you want me to do? Ask if he needs help with his shopping?" Truman sniped.

"I don't expect you to understand this or sympathise in any way but I thought you might recognise the importance of this for me if nothing else." Letting this remark linger in the air for a few moments, she then added, "You can't let the past tie you down or cloud your judgment forever, Truman. You are still responsible for the welfare of this community."

Great, the guilt card.

"He's a monster, Lorraine." Truman had no other retort.

"He may be. Or may *have* been. But that does not alter the fact that he is my patient and I have a duty of care for him now. I am so close, Truman," her voice starting to crack as the emotion flooded to her eyes. This case had been seen as a culmination of her own rising career. If someone would just give her the time and understanding she needed to break Dexler's surface and find what she believed lived within his tortured shell; a scared, misunderstood boy who for years and hidden in fear of those around him.

"I need you," she finally admitted.

Truman pondered her words for a second longer than he intended.

"I have raised, moulded this force on fighting for the truth, regardless of how many times we are told we are wrong. To show a willingness to acknowledge or aid this man"s welfare would betray all of that and cast doubt over my commitment and loyalties. Not to mention my character. I simply can't do that, Lorraine," Then his voice softened, "I'm sorry."

An awkward silence was followed by an even more uncomfortable reply.

"Okay Truman. I'm sorry to have bothered you. I should have known better than to ask." Truman instantly regretted his decision.

And not for the first time in his chequered career, he reached into the small drawer at the bottom of his desk and pulled out the hip flask.

*****

Lorraine held the handset to her ear for a few moments after the click of the receiver at the other end. Truman had been her only hope, but she now cursed herself for asking him. Had she forgotten how hard it was for him to hear the name Colin Dexler? Now she felt like a fool. Was she becoming too immersed in this case? What was the harm in just sitting back and waiting for Colin to call her when he was ready? Or maybe he was genuinely running late.

But for some reason she had the feeling that something was not right. Colin was not the most vocal of her patients and some days their sessions had been no more successful than getting him to answer two or three of her questions. Patience was what was needed to understand this poor man and she seemed to be the only one willing to give her time to help him.

Truman remained sore that his investigation had been fruitless, even though he believed he'd come close to the truth. She wondered if maybe she was the only one that had gotten close to really discovering the truth of Colin Dexler's condition. She had seen him stricken with fear a few times whilst in her office, scared of a being he referred to as The Reaper.

He had been severely traumatised as a young child because of the actions of an abusive father and in his mind he may still be that child hiding in the closet.

She pressed the buzzer on the intercom situated on her desk.

"Yes, doctor?" came the chirpy reply from the other end.

"Don't suppose there has been any word from Mr. Dexler?"

"No, I'm afraid not. Would you like me to try ringing his house again?"

"No, no." Lorraine answered, "I don't suppose he would answer after the last attempt anyway. I am just popping down for a smoke and to catch the breeze before my twelve o"clock. Could you come down and get me if you hear anything please, April?"

"Of course. May I suggest taking your jacket down with you? It's mighty chilly out there."

Lorraine thanked her but ignored the suggestion. The cold air would help wake her mind and clear her head of the worries about her patient. Truman had always told her that she was too married to her work. She would never be able to live with the guilt of letting anyone down who was in her care.

That's rich, coming from him.

But he was right.

Dr. Thacker pulled back the top drawer of her heavy, oak desk and took out the remains of that morning's pack of menthol cigarettes. If she must smoke, she tried to make the best choice as far as her taste buds went. Returning to her telephone she put it on Do Not Disturb before leaving her office.

*****

As soon as she exited the double doors of the main lobby at Wildermoor Psychiatric Institute, Lorraine couldn't help raising her arms, wrapping them across at the elbows and trying to stop as much heat escaping as she could. April was right; she should have worn her jacket. Lorraine always loved the winter though. The air seemed fresher and the grass crunched underfoot. With the colder months first came the joy and celebration of Christmas – this year spent by herself with only her cat, Ryker, for company; she had chosen not to make the trip back to London to spend the holidays with her overbearing, overprotective and over-eager family.

She no longer minded being alone. Before she had met Truman Darke she had always craved company and attention, especially from the opposite sex. Their relationship and their break-up had left her with a new confidence that she could survive on her own. From that moment she had decided to commit herself to her career.

The breakdown of the love affair coincided with both the end (nay, the *failing*) of Truman's attempts to convict Colin Dexler and likewise her acquisition of the accused man as her newest client. She had known how much the case and its result had affected Truman and when he told her that he needed space for himself she did not argue. The relationship would have been doomed from that point, anyway.

That's why the Dexler appointment had been so important for her. It presented her with an opportunity to be the one to right the wrongs that the Wildermoor PD had bestowed upon him. It was going to be a new start for her and Colin, too.

But she had to admit that Truman's attitude towards her plea for help had left her shaken, She felt she had woken up a sleeping beast that had lived deep within him for the last six months. The memories, not to mention the humiliation, were still fresh in his mind and seeing the woman he had loved siding with the devil had been too much for him to bear.

Lorraine managed to prise her arms apart for long enough to reach into the half-empty packet of cigarettes, remove the first she laid a finger on and quickly rest it between her lips. She wrestled with the chilled air to ignite the lighter in her hand. She welcomed the burst of warmth from the flame as she brought it to her mouth.

She inhaled deeply and felt her body sag as she relaxed; savouring each subsequent small drag she took. The Institute was situated just on the corner of the main high street, at the point where the retail units ended and the housing estate began. As a result of the close proximity of the centre to the houses there was very little in the way of through-traffic in this part of the village.

When she first moved to Wildermoor she had thought it odd that a village of this size warranted its own Psychiatric Centre. But after a few short weeks, with the dozens of patients that had passed through her doors, she no longer questioned it. Wildermoor was home to many characters, all with their own secrets, horrors and fears. This place had a history and you only had to listen to the sounds of the lives that passed by to realise this. The silence told the worst story of all.

A twig snapped somewhere behind her.

She was so lost in her own thoughts that the sudden sound made her jump. Immediately embarrassed, she shyly looked away from the couple of practitioners walking towards the lobby from the rear courtyard entrance.

She then heard a soft, low dragging along the ground for a few seconds. Then nothing.

Surely an animal scurrying to find shelter in the boundary bushes around the grounds, she reasoned.

Just then a feeling overcame her that a pair of eyes was boring into her back.

She turned her head with a start and thought she saw a shadow dart through the bushes from the courtyard to the shaded rear entrance to the Institute building.

Chapter Eight

Thomas Laing woke with a start, his body stiffened and he drew in a short sharp breath. When he fell into deep slumbers his breathing had a tendency to slow to such a point that he actually managed to skip breaths. A cold shiver coursed through him, so deeply that his chest felt as though it were taking in iced water. He frantically strained his eyes to focus on the clock face on the centre of the dash as his blurred vision began to clear.

12:49pm. His body clock had woken him just in time. He had exactly sixty seconds to rouse himself fully before starting the short walk back to the station.

He rubbed his eyes and pulled at his face to speed up the process. He froze when he noticed the figure standing only a couple of feet away from his window. A frozen stare and cold eyes penetrated the glass. The dead eyes staring at Laing made him instantly feel uneasy, threatened.

The figure seemed to be suspended, lifeless and staring. It's mouth moving only slightly enough for Laing to determine that he was muttering something to himself. His eyes never moving or flickering away from where he sat in his elderly Astra.

Laing began to turn the stiff handle to his right, the windows straining down within their frame. Laing was about to call out to the man unsure whether he was going to ask if he was okay or what his bloody problem was. The man remained seemingly lifeless, his shoulders sagged and his body hanging limply. His face stared dumbly, suggesting nothing was going on in his mind.

Laing's own breathing became shallow as he started to make out odd words from the man's mutterings.

"You…what…are…you?" The strange man mumbled breathlessly, almost incoherently.

Just then his eyes flickered back to life as if an invisible force had reached behind him and turned his power back on. His dead eyes whirred into life, darting quickly from side to side as his body turned and shuffled down the side street adjoining Exeter Street out of sight.

Laing was feeling more at ease until he noticed the object hanging from the figure's right hand. Any closer to the ground and it would have been dragged along the uneven concrete; from his hand hung a foot-long, heavy-duty wrench.

As the figure disappeared around the corner, the wrench left behind a trail of blood that looked like a wet shadow.

Chapter Nine

"Good morning, Mr Sheppard," April greeted the stout gentleman as he approached her desk making an audible shivering noise letting her know that he felt the chill outside. She glanced up at the wall clock as she said it checking it was indeed still morning. 11:57am to be exact. She was satisfied she had not made a faux-pas.

"Good morning to you, Miss Jones," he beamed back, "Lovely weather this time of year, isn't it?"

She smiled and nodded in agreement.

Graham Sheppard could always lighten the dullest of mornings with his cheery smile and witty banter. April had often wondered why he needed to see Dr. Thacker at all, given his perpetual good moods. She had not been privy to that information, of course, due to doctor-patient confidentiality. One of her earlier theories that she had since dismissed was that Thacker was dishing out an extra type of therapy to a lucky few.

"Dr. Thacker has just popped out for a quick break, but please feel free to make yourself comfortable," she told him signalling the available comfy chairs arranged in the waiting area. "The new copy of Caravanning Weekly arrived this morning," she said knowing that this was one of the perks Mr. Sheppard had been afforded for being Lorraine's very first and longest-serving client.

He smiled warmly and eagerly made his way to the lounge, slipping off his green raincoat and hanging it on the coat stand in the corner. He sank into a chair – the usual one on the furthest right, nearest Dr. Thacker's office and picked up the magazine from the arrangement on the coffee table.

Such a pleasant man, April always thought. No mention of a Mrs. Sheppard during any of their brief conversations. His contentment at small graces such as conversations about the weather, the latest cricket results and caravanning were refreshing. He did not seem to have any problems that warranted the need for psychological counselling on a regular basis. But then again, she was beginning to learn that one never knew what went on below the surface.

When April next glanced at the surgery's wall clock it was 12:06pm. Dr. Thacker had still not returned. It was not unusual for her to get distracted whilst on a cigarette break. It would require her to bump into one of the resident nurses reporting for the next shift so April returned to her PC monitor and proceeded to carry on updating the current patient records, as was tradition at that time of day.

12:17pm came and still the Dr. had not breezed through Reception apologising for her tardiness in timekeeping. April looked across at Mr Sheppard who, by now, had read the last few pages of his magazine. She could sense he was getting a little tetchy as he glanced in her direction hoping for an update or explanation.

"I'm awfully sorry for the wait, sir. I can't think what is keeping Dr. Thacker so long."

"It's quite alright, Miss Jones," he replied too politely, trying to mask his annoyance, "I'm sure she won't be long."

April nodded but as her gaze returned to the spreadsheet on her screen she could not help glancing at the door. She did not want to appear nervous or concerned in anyway, as some patients were liable to become anxious at the first sense of fear, but she was becoming deeply worried. Lorraine was not one to keep her clients waiting without rescheduling appointments or getting a message to April.

"I might just pop to the store room a second, if that is okay Mr Sheppard? I seem to have run out of printer paper."

Not waiting for his nod of acceptance, she left her desk and proceeded down the short hallway. With Mr Sheppard's attention on the magazine as he flicked through the pages for a second time, he did not see her turn right instead of left and head out of the door through the lobby.

Chapter Ten

He knew that the shivers would stop. He had to keep telling himself that it was just the cold cutting through him causing him to shake. It had not exactly gone to plan but he had no choice. He had prepared himself mentally to expect one not two. *That was her fault, not mine.*

Upon reaching the gate of the rear courtyard entrance to the Institute, Dexler had almost been caught by a couple of jovial nurses on their way to start their shift. He managed to catch snippets of their inane conversation as they passed. When he slipped through the next gated entrance at the front of the clinic he saw her standing there. He could only see the back of her head and the wisps of smoke lifting from above her but he knew it was Dr. Thacker.

One of the nurses caught the doctor's attention so that Dexler had to quickly change his direction and dive around the nearest corner of the building, where the lobby jutted out from the menacing construction. He followed the shadows until he came to a service door, a dead end.

He had to retrace his steps and retreat; he had already failed and hated himself for it.

He would never be free from Him, *It.*

He managed to get within four feet of the end of the small alleyway down which he had descended before she appeared in front of him. She stopped dead in her tracks then started talking but he could not hear or understand the sounds coming from her mouth. God, why didn't she talk properly? Was she not schooled enough to separate words from becoming mere sounds? *Academic my arse. They're all the same. They all think they're better than me just for having an education.*

She took a step closer to Dexler. Suddenly his arm flinched and rose above his head. Her eyes traced the weapon he held high. Dumbfounded by what she was seeing, the doctor was unable to raise an alarm, signal for help or defend herself. It was probably for the best that she had no time to resist. The blow would have shattered her wrist had she tried to block it.

Dexler had aimed perfectly and the first shot shattered her skull, damaging her brain so that it shut off on impact. It dulled her senses to the other four blows that Dexler rained down, the wrench now coated in a film of blood that flowed freely from Lorraine Thacker's head.

Her body twitched a few times more and then ceased. Ceased to breathe, ceased to be. The silence set in and suddenly Dexler could breathe easy again. His senses were so keen he could even smell the flowers that grew nearby, that were growing freely, straining from under the chain-link fence that bordered the rear of the building to the courtyard beyond. Daisies? Tulips? He was not sure and did not care. Suddenly he felt free, as if some blockage in his sinuses and mind had suddenly been dislodged.

The Reaper had come to him through her. His hulking shadowy form had appeared from around the corner with her. That's why the decision to strike them down had come so easily without remorse or panic. Now he looked around and The Reaper was nowhere to be seen. He could no longer feel him. He could no longer smell the stench of his crisp flesh. At last he was free.

He had been unwise though and let his guard down for a moment. Suddenly another woman had appeared – he recognised her as the doctor's receptionist - finding him standing in a growing pool of fresh blood and the limp, battered body of her employer at his feet.

She didn't have time to scream out and summon the shadows to take him away, before he brought his trusted metal friend along her left cheek, smashing her jaw in a number of places. A strangled groan escaped from her as she slumped to the floor, instinctively clutching the side of her face he had just ruined. Her eyes met his and he could sense the pleading in her stare. Her eyes grew wider as he brought the wrench down one last time across her temple.

*****

He fled the scene too quickly for his age and condition. The journey home seemed never-ending but once he had slowed his pace and controlled his breathing, he felt at peace.

Even in his ever-deepening madness, Colin Dexler knew that he could not run forever and that now they would come for him. It had all happened so fast that he barely had time to conceal the bodies. Once the alarm was raised they would soon find them. The dead weight of Dr. Thacker, who he had seen to first, had sapped all of his strength. He lifted her up and folded her into the nearby empty recycling bin. How often did they empty their bins anyway? For all he knew she could be in there for a week before being found.

The second body might give him away. Dexler had been overcome with shortness of breath, dizziness, nausea and fatigue. He could only manage to drag the corpse to the rear of the building and heave it under the bordering hedge. The low-hanging leaves would only conceal so much of her and he was unable to get her right leg to stay curled up in its position over the left enough to hold it in place.

Everything started to appear clear to him as he approached the turning for Exeter Street. He had taken a detour to try and clear his head and just in case anyone had already picked up his trail. He had forgotten to wipe down and dispose of the weapon he still carried and that left a dripping trail behind him.

In any event the sun was starting to break through, not enough to warm the air as his breath remained visible, but it was a start. The street was quiet; most of the residents already at work or those who laboured their day away in front of the TV were still in bed. Dexler could not abide the lazy. His father had made him scared of having spare time for spare time was when the trouble usually started.

It was during those quiet moments that He would haunt him too.

But those days were gone now that Dr. Thacker had been taken care of. Suddenly he felt a ton-weight had been lifted from his chest and shoulders, one he had carried around with him since he was seven years old. That was until the moment that he approached the battered Vauxhall parked shy of the corner, feet away from where he turned to walk down the side street to where his own house stood.

As he drew closer, his chest felt heavier, pressured. He struggled to breathe as he looked in through the window of the car. The smell was quickly rising through his nostrils so that he could taste the burnt, rotten meat at the back of his throat. A retch rose from the pit of his stomach and, as he stared into the cab of the car, the shadow man appeared on the opposite side of the car and loomed menacingly over it, staring straight at the man inside.

For the first time the shadow man's stare was not fixed on Dexler. Why then could Colin still not breathe?

*****

Dexler remained frozen to the spot as he watched The Reaper move around the side of the car trying to find a way in.

He seemed transfixed on the figure that lay asleep inside the vehicle. Dexler could tell that The Reaper *wanted* the sleeping man. His movements became more agitated. His head turned frantically from left to right, as he adjusted his body to try and gain access to the car; one hand pressed on the passenger window the other was planted on the windscreen.

For years Dexler had kept the secret of The Reaper to himself. He could not face the ridicule of being haunted by a phantom. And the few people to whom he had divulged this apparition, Dr. Thacker included, had been quick to pass it off as a symptom of psychiatric trauma; representing the abusive father in Dexler's own twisted, terrifying world. But for all of this time The Reaper had existed as flesh, blood and bone to him. He had *felt* him. He smelt his presence every time he appeared and the fear was overwhelming.

But now The Reaper looked strangely human, vulnerable, in his attempt to break through a structure he had not met before, his gesticulations illustrating his frustration.

It was the way The Reaper was wanting, lusting over the sleeping man that was so disturbing. Colin had never seen The Reaper display any attributes or emotions like that around him. What did the sleeping man have that Colin didn't?

Instantly, Dexler hated the sleeping man. He wanted to show The Reaper how to break into the car, how to physically break another person just as The Reaper had broken him after all these years. Fear gave way to some form of masochistic jealousy.

The Reaper was to blame for everything – for the grisly death of his parents, the sickening procedures that Dexler had had to perform to break down their bodies and dispose of the flesh and then the bones, the unimaginable torture he had had to perform on the unwelcome visitors that turned up unexpectedly the day before Wildemroor's finest had found Colin and taken him away. But The Reaper had, in some way, made Dexler feel special, wanted, maybe even important to

Him. Dr Thacker was to blame for bringing The Reaper back to him, so therefore *it* was also responsible for her death and that of her receptionist.

The sleeping man obviously had a link to this phantom also. The death of Dr. Thacker was supposed to have dispelled The Reaper from Dexler's life for good, but no – this man had also been sent to torment Dexler. Why couldn't everyone just leave him alone?   Why couldn't The Reaper just stop tormenting him?

The Reaper's actions became more frenzied, until finally it turned to face Dexler. Its body tensed and seemed to grow a full foot taller and from within its heavy dark hood came a sound more guttural than any he had heard before, more grating than any fingers on a chalkboard. The force of this outcry rooted Dexler to the spot, his breathing stopped in an instant.

But still Dexler struggled to shout back at the shadow.

"Why are you doing this?" He screamed. "Who are you? What do you want from me?! Why can't you just leave me alone? I DON"T NEED YOU!"

He heard the words perfectly in his mind, but his mouth had frozen and only a few of his muttered words grew sound.

The street that lay behind The Reaper started to shimmer, like the hottest summer day shone its rays on the tarmac road. The shimmering became a trembling, until soon he felt a series of tremors taking place in the world behind the phantom.

Flames appeared from under the Vauxhall Astra licking the paintwork. They grew until they slithered up the doors and the windows. The Reaper stood within the blaze, his arms stretched out before him, reaching towards Dexler. Colin wanted to scream but the heat had dried his throat. It felt as though his heart was slowing and his lungs were shutting down. The world before Dexler started to fade as he started to lose consciousness.   He could feel his skin starting to tighten as it blistered. It would not be long before the skin would peel back on itself as he was burnt alive. Was that the destiny that the Reaper had in store for him? Surely not.

Within a flash the heat died and the air held in Dexler's lungs expelled in a gasp. The flames were gone, the Vauxhall before him appeared as it was before, not burnt.

Dexler's eyes began to focus on the houses stretched out in a neat line either side of him The simple stone cladding on the opposite side of the street shone a brilliant white as the emerging sunlight hit them.

Dexler looked once more into the car. The Reaper was no longer pressed against the windscreen. He was gone.

The sleeping man however had awoken and was staring back at Dexler.

Thomas Laing looked menacingly at Colin Dexler; a Cheshire-cat smile growing across his face, his tongue slithered out from his thin lips and ran along the top row of perfect teeth. His cold blue eyes did not move and something told him they could not be trusted.

The familiar feeling of dread and pure fear swept over Dexler. It was the same he had felt every day of his miserable life since he had hidden in his closet as a small child.

Dexler quickly turned and ran down the side street. He did not stop until he got to his front door five houses down. He fumbled with the key in the lock. *Please don't fail, not now.* The keys fell to the floor. With a trembling hand Dexler tried again, this time the key sliding easily into the lock. With a swift turn and push on the door Dexler fell into his hallway and slammed the door.

For the next hour Colin Dexler wept until he fell asleep.

Chapter Eleven

He woke up surrounded by darkness but Dexler knew that he was not at home. This place felt different, alien to him. The air was humid. He could smell the earth so strongly he felt that he was surrounded by it. Had he been buried alive and woken up in his own grave? As he got to his feet he realised this could not be the case.

A single flamed torch on the wall sparked and lit as if on command, illuminating the small area in which Dexler stood. It was not an empty tomb as he had first feared. The room was small, maybe no more than ten feet square and consisted of a few simple items of furniture. A low, thin framed bed sat behind him, a heavy oak wardrobe to his right and a beautifully carved wooden dressing table before him. On the top of the table was a mirror, the main panel of reflective glass sitting central to two smaller ones hinged on either side allowing them to fold away if the reflection became too much to bear. A small amount of light shed by the flame shone back from the mirrors so Colin could see his own face staring back at him. He walked closer to the ornate table.

He could tell he was dreaming the moment he saw his face. In his dreams his appearance was a lot more favourable. His skin appeared supple and possessed a healthy glow, the bags from under his eyes had lifted and he looked rested, at peace.

At no point was there evidence of the years of sleepless nights and neglect that he had suffered for so long. Even his hair was thicker; the grey flecks replaced by a black dusting, making him look ten years younger.

Where the hell was he? This was not his house yet he felt strangely at home as if this was somewhere he knew. Suddenly a voice appeared out of the darkness behind him, as soft as the lamplight.

"There is no need to worry anymore, Colin." Dexler jumped at first but then started to feel at ease once more. "He will harm you no more."

Dexler turned his head to search the sea of darkness behind him from which a small, yet commanding presence emerged. The man stood no more than five-and-a-half feet tall, silver hair, cleanly shaven and dressed in the most beautiful white gown he had ever seen. Not a lifeless sheet acting as a nightgown but a heavy robe of quality that gave this man a sense of standing.

The man recognised the puzzled look on Dexler's face.

`You know of whom I speak." The man said.

"What do you know of me?"

"As much as I need to know and possibly more than you know of yourself."

Colin looked around the room balking at the last remark. It was cosy, he had to admit that. Not even in his own house or his own bed had he felt so calm for many years. More than he cared to remember.

"You still fear him," the elder continued, "but you need not. He has moved on to another subject now." The flippant use of the word subject sent a shiver down Colin's back. Had he been no more than a subject himself? "There is a new hope."

"A new hope? For whom exactly?"

"Us!" came the surprised reply as if the question was ridiculous. "We have all been waiting for a new gateway to open."

Colin decided that the man spoke only in riddles and found no sense in the answers he was getting. He was now convinced this was all a creation of his own imagination, a surreal yet safe world that his subconscious had created, waiting for this moment to invite him in. There was no threat in there and nothing to fear.

He closed his eyes for a few moments taking in the smells and sounds of the enigmatic cavern, whilst also testing his theory that he was in fact dreaming. When he re-opened his eyes, he was looking once more into the mirror and the old man stood behind him looking at Dexler through the reflection as he spoke. Dexler blocked out his words by focusing on the other sounds around him, of which there were few besides a regular, rhythmic humming that appeared to emanate from the core of the room in which he stood.

"What is this place?" Colin asked finally.

"It is any place you want it to be but in reality is the last place you hoped it would be." Great, he thought, another riddle. "All you need to know is that he cannot harm you here."

Colin knew what this meant, but wanted to block the phantom from his mind.

"You talk of him as if he is real," he challenged.

"And you don't think so? You – the man who has been running scared of him almost your whole life. You - who has let himself be influenced and manipulated by him, in order to commit sins against others in his name - question his existence?" Dexler could tell he had started to test the nerve of this man, whoever he was. "Or were you simply looking for someone to blame for your *own* sins?"

Dexler stared into the mirror chastised, at first unable to respond. The reflection altered to show a great fire, the sounds of torturous pain hidden within. The picture became clearer until he knew he recognised the house that was being devoured by the flames. He suddenly realised that the mirror was replaying scenes of his own tortured memories.

The humming sound became more of a pulse, growing louder as Dexler started into the fire once more.

*****

"No-one ever wanted to believe me when I spoke of him," Dexler said, his voice breaking as he struggled to hold back tears. He sat perched on one of the end corners of the small cot, vulnerable. The old man remained where he stood, body not moving, hands clasped together, looking down at Dexler's sorry form. The strength he had exuded when he had first seen himself in the mirror had begun to fade and he was shrinking back within his true self. "When they found me at the house as it burned, and I said it wasn't me, that a man of shadow had caused it, they looked at me as if I were confessing my guilt. I had no guilt for the crime, as I didn't commit it."

"Nor did you feel guilt or remorse for the death of your father that day," the old man offered.

Dexler bowed his head in an act that could have been perceived of shame, had it not been for the slimy smile that slithered over his lips.

"He had it coming," he returned, for the first time sounding like the criminal he had been labelled as.

"Maybe, but does the moral and criminal standing of one justify the acts of another?" This was not a question that required, nor received, a response. "Your whole life has been spent trying to find excuses for your sins and others to blame. Is that why you are so unsure of His existence now? Do you think you are at last facing up to your own role in all of your crimes?"

He was being tested, Colin thought, that was all. This was merely a rehearsal for when the police finally found him. His time would be up soon, that was unavoidable, but he was not about to show weakness.

"For so long I have been told that He doesn't exist," Colin responded calmly and with conviction, "that he is merely a product of my traumatic youth." The last two words were spat rather than spoken.

"Is that what you believe or simply what you had been *led* to believe? How can you be so sure of yourself now?"

"Madness exists merely in those around us; not in our own minds. You – *this* – are merely a product of my own cognitions."

The old man smiled coldly. It was at this point that Colin noticed something strange and unnerving about the figure. Two dark, empty spheres rested where his eyes should have been. Life seemed to exude from this man everywhere else but his eyes, the windows to his soul, were pitch black.

"Who are you?" Colin asked breathlessly.

"Who I am and where you are is not important. It is not why you are here, if you even believe you are here at all."

Colin shook his head and his gaze shifted to the floor. He couldn't look at those empty pits any longer.

"I do not know where I am anymore."

"You are where you belong."

The pulsing in the background was now getting stronger, resonating deep inside Dexler's ears and burrowing into his mind. He felt his head throb, the pain in his temples flaring with each beat.

"What is that sound? What is this place?" he pleaded.

"Neither is important" the man replied coldly.

Colin covered his ears with his hands, pushing tightly against them to block out the pulsing that was ringing in his mind, making it ache. The throbbing of this sound started to ease as the thrum slowed. Almost reduced to tears, Colin repeated

"Madness exists merely in those around us; not in our own minds. Madness exists merely in those around us; not in our own minds." His body started to rock back and forth on the spot as he spoke to himself.

"You're wrong," said the old man, "I of all men know that."

"Who *are* you?" Colin asked again. "Please make it stop," he begged referring to the humming sound.

"It will cease when it is ready," he replied. "As for me, in life my name was Julius Archibald."

"What do you want from me?"

"I am here to tell you that you need not fear him anymore. He is done with you."

As the nauseating sound and sensations of the throbbing began to ease, Colin's mind returned to thoughts of the sleeping man in the car, the one who had evoked that animalistic and desperate reaction from The Reaper. The anger began to rise once more.

"What does he have that I don't?"

"Strength," the reply was blunt and honest. "Desire. He – *we*- need these in order to succeed, to live again and rule as we once should have. These attributes are easy to manipulate. Your weakness was your weakness alone. He, our Leader, merely leeched from you, living from the evil inside of you and that which came through the acts you committed, but he could not gain strength from you for you are weak."

It was all becoming clearer for Colin. Finally he understood why he had been haunted for so long. The Reaper latched onto those who were vulnerable and easy to control, puppeteering in the hope that his power may grow with or through them. The more Colin reacted to his presence and acted on the emotions he felt - the anger, the resentment, the joy from bringing pain to others – he was displaying weakness, unable to control his baser instincts, and allowing himself to be manipulated by something that others could not see.

As Colin's head rose from his hands, the pulsing suddenly ceased. He looked up to find Julius Archibald gazing at the ceiling. A warm smile, yet chilling in its appearance, broke over Archibald's face.

"What is it?" Colin asked, trembling.

"It has begun," Archibald replied, his gaze returning to Dexler. "They are coming for you. Goodbye Colin."

Dexler tentatively rose from the cot and stared at what was taking place on the floor before him. The shadows that had formed, flickered from the light of the single torch and started shifting, crawling towards him. They rose up from the floor and stood in front of him. Everywhere he turned, more and more of the shadows were lining the room, now resembling a cell. They appeared like a demonic firing squad, watching and waiting to strike. As Colin followed each apparition, more features started to form on them all; some grew faces that grimaced, displaying sickening deformities. Others formed limbs that had been cut short. One hunched over and resembled an unholy impression of something wolf-like.

Colin felt that he knew them all and that he was somehow the source of all of their agony. They all crept forward towards him; those who had arms reached them out grabbing, tearing, and slicing him. His screams curdled within his cavernous cell. With one last frantic look around the space, he realised that there was no door, no windows, no ceiling. No way out.

The pulsing started again as the shadows tore Colin's body, ribboning his flesh, his screams weakening to pathetic whimpers. The pulsing shook the walls and were splitting Colin's head from within, the sounds becoming louder and faster.

In the dark, cold, lonely hallway of his house, Colin Dexler's body laid slumped upright against the front door, not moving.

The pounding on the door grew louder as the shouted requests became frantic orders.

"Wildermoor Police, open up!" the officer shouted, rattling the weak wooden door with every slam of his fist. "I know you"re in there, Dexler. This time we have you," screamed DI Darke.

The rhythmic, pulsing of Dexler"s heart slowed and finally stopped. As he remained locked, trapped, inside his broken mind learning the truth that he had sought for so long, his life slipped away. Inside his dying body, his soul was being torn apart. The demons within him were hungry, and finally able to feed.

Chapter Twelve

Thomas Laing slowed his feet and his breathing to a more sensible pace and made the most of the walk from HQ to his car to clear his head. It had been a day that he would rather, but was unlikely to, forget. The unwanted voyeur from his lunch break played on his mind all day. The trail that he had seen dripping from the tool he saw hanging from the man''s hand had disappeared by the time Laing made it out of his car. The man was nowhere to be seen. Could it be that he had not fully awoken from his slumber and his mind was simply playing tricks on him?

As he made it to his car and unlocked the driver's door – no central locking on that bad boy – he was instantly stopped by a strange sensation. He raised his hand and gently rubbed his temple to relieve the sudden tension there. Might be the start of a migraine, he thought. He suffered them infrequently but severely and wouldn't normally drive but knew walking would be just as uncomfortable. *Best stop off into the nearest supermarket pharmacy on the way home and have an early night*, he decided.

Despite the stop off, he was home within half an hour. The entrance to Wisbourne Avenue always pleased him. Its gentle sweeping turns made a change from the one-direction and ninety-degree-turn main road which led from the centre of the village. The developers, in their vision to create the warm welcoming retreat for its residents, had planted willow trees on each bend. They seemed to enhance to majesty of these winter months.

Laing proudly parked the Astra on his driveway as he did every night. It may not be long before he would have to give up the ghost of his father's trusted automobile. Throughout the whole journey home, the car had filled with a smell of burning. He couldn't decide what it was. Could be anything from the fan belt to the tyres or even just dust that had settled in the air circulation unit.

His headache had not eased and at 6:20pm the darkening sky and oncoming headlights had not helped. The usual post-dinner whiskey was probably not on the cards tonight.

Laing was soon inside the warmth of his hallway but tonight he could not bear to turn the lights on. The street lamp outside shone just enough illumination in through the frosted windows of the front door so that he could make his way to the kitchen. He poured himself a glass of water, located the box of painkillers from his pocket and knocked two back before retreating to the lounge through the open archway leading from the kitchen.

Instead of his usual routine of switching on the standard lamp he by-passed his recliner and walked towards the drinks cabinet on the opposite side of the room. He had already justified one night cap before he had closed the front door.

"The Devil's drink," a voice muttered in the darkness. Laing spun round still not able to make out much in the dark. "Make it two," the voice continued, "we have much to talk about."

*****

Laing stared into the shadows in disbelief. He was sure he had not left his house without locking up this morning. Of course he hadn't. He had unlocked the door himself only two minutes earlier. He was a cautious man. *No, this man must have crept in behind me when I walked in then.* But he had closed the door after only a few seconds of being in the house. No grown man could move that lightly that Laing would not have heard him. He would definitely have heard something.

He strained to look towards his leather recliner chair trying to make out any shape at all but the harder he strained his eyes the darker the room became. He quickly blinked two or three times to release the tension but the figure still did not materialise.

Suddenly he heard the creak of the leather upholstery as it shifted below its body. Laing was too confused to even reach over to his left and turn on the small table lamp on top of the drinks cabinet. Although he could not make out the man who had invaded his home, he knew he had heard that voice before.

"I told you never to come after me again," he mustered with shortening breath, attempting to maintain a sense of calmness.

"That is beyond my control," the voice replied, its voice low, rasping, each word sounding like a struggle but deliberate in its delivery, "I have told you before."

"You promised me that I was finished with this shit."

With a trembling hand Laing removed the stopper from the crystal decanter and poured a measure of whiskey into his tumbler. He did not bother to measure since it would not be his last.

"Your destiny was written for you long ago, you cannot change that. Not even I have the power to prevent it. We are so close."

"Who is this *we?* I'm not party to any of this. I didn"t ask for it and I owe you nothing," His voice rising but audibly shaking.

"The *we* is not important now. What is important are the things that you can achieve here if you only open up and stop resisting what is coming," the man said rising from his chair. Laing could feel him walk towards where he stood and could finally make out the shape of the intruder who was not a stranger. He stood shorter than Laing at only five-foot-six, and his build did not appear to possess any strength. Physical ability aside, a sense of awe overcame Laing; the feeling of being in the presence of some higher power. His arguments and resistance to this man would not get him far; he knew that but could not accept it.

This man - and those who follow him - had invaded his life before. Years ago, when Laing was a child, they were apparitions that haunted his dreams but they had now become figures who stalked his days.

"How did you find me?" He asked, unsure if he wanted to know the answer.

"We have our means," the answer was stern. "Why can't you just accept it? You and He are now one. He led us to you and his strength will continue to grow. But you need to do your bit too now. We have set the wheels in motion and those who need to be…*helped*… out of our way, must be taken care of."

"You mean Truman?" Laing asked. For the first time since leaving the station his mind was cast back to his employer. Laing had witnessed a sad occurrence that every ambitious young man dreads seeing; when a mentor - a hero - is reduced to the barest of emotions; rage and despair. He had never seen a man broken so easily as when he witnessed Truman being informed of the bodies found behind Wildermoor Brook. Truman knew, as did the rest of the department, the minute that Commissioner Roberts came to the office involuntarily to discuss "recent developments," that it could only be bad news.

Truman's reaction had been just what the Commissioner had expected and feared would be from his commanding officer. He had come to the meeting prepared. Truman was not only kept off the ensuing murder investigation due to his acquaintance with one of the victims, Lorraine Thacker, but he was suspended from his position for its duration, cited as "unfit to carry out his duties." Truman could not meet the stares of any of his colleagues, many of them his students, as he was escorted from the station.

"Haven't we done enough to him already? He's no longer a problem."

"Truman Darke is not who he seems," the voice stated. "It is time to ensure that he does not become more than a simple hindrance." Laing felt the man"s cold hand reach towards his and hand him an unsealed envelope.

"You will attend a meeting with Commisioner Roberts tomorrow at 8am. You will call him in two hours' time, saying that you have in your possession evidence to show that Truman is going after Dexler himself. This is the letter, the proof. You will urge him to send officers to check it out. The night patrol will be dispatched in force to Dexler's house. They will find Dexler dead and Truman on the scene, at which time he will be arrested and taken into custody." Laing wanted to cover his ears like a child singing to himself as he did so, as he listened to the sickening plans – the orders – he was being given.

"Tomorrow morning, you will give him the letter. Truman will stand trial for the murder of Colin Dexler, with no motive, except that of blind rage, hate and the influence of alcohol. Truman will be locked up. He will longer be of our concern." The man leaned in closer towards Laing and put a bony hand on his shoulder. "You know what this will mean for us."

The figure brushed past Laing and lingered in the doorway leading back out into the entrance hall. When it turned back towards him, Laing could only trace the outline of the shadowy shape as it drew its shoulders back and tilted its head higher.

"You are destined for great things, *Thomas*," said the man, emphasising the name as if it were only an alleged moniker.

Laing glanced down at the envelope that he held in his hand and glanced back up at the shadowy figure. He could make out more of the contours of its bony face, skin drawn and hanging limp. The years had not been kind to this soul, Laing observed. The one disturbing feature was the absence of his eyes. Instead there were two pits that seemed to grow darker than any of the corners of his unlit living room. They were sucking all life and light into themselves to be lost forever.

"Yes, Father," he said, his head bowed, the shame of what he was to do bearing down on his shoulders. He knew how Atlas felt carrying the world on his back. The hopes and future of this new society, this new religion, this new world – this Hell - that Father Archibald was planning, that he had told Laing he had been planning for centuries, rested on him.

He looked down at the envelope one more time before looking back towards the doorway to find the figure had gone. Laing could make out the ascending staircase on the far wall through the open door. The figure had vanished without a trace like it had all those years ago.

Laing hurriedly switched on the lamp to his left on top of the drinks cabinet then looked back at the hallway to make sure that he was once again alone.

The envelope was addressed to him and he recognised the scripture in which it had been written. He took the sheet of paper from within and held it beneath the light beside him.

Thomas,
Things have turned against me and I fear that they will turn this force into a circus. I need to know whom I can trust.
Meet me at 33 Exeter Street tonight at 9pm.
I need justice. And I need your help.
Regards,
DI Truman Darke.

Simple, Laing thought as he stared once more at the letter. That's how it was meant to be. So why now did he feel a cold stabbing in the pit of his stomach? Wildermoor was supposed to be his new start but now his past and future were playing out side-by-side in his mind.

He poured himself another double measure and swallowed it in one, grimacing as the warmth coursed down his throat, welcoming the distraction for even the briefest of moments and hoping the fuzziness would set in soon.

He finally collapsed into the waiting leather recliner, whose arms welcomed him and enveloped him in a warm embrace. He felt safe at last. His headache was returning, his vision starting to blur and colourful spots danced before his eyes. He squinted towards the red glowing digits of the clock display on his VCR.

There were two hours before he had to make the call. He poured himself another drink.

*****

Laing's hands would not stop shaking and he fumbled with the telephone handset as he rested it back on the receiver. His stomach was turning like never before; he felt physically sick. He put it down to too much whiskey. *I have done the right thing. This is my destiny, after all…* He needed had to suck it up and be a man. His twenty-two years would not have been wasted. He would be a god in ten more. That was the plan. *Nobody else has a life plan like that,* he thought as he slowly stood, raising his head. Suddenly he felt an overwhelming power running through his body, like his blood carried some kind of opiate that made him invincible.

He looked at the curtains adorning the front bay window and watched the shadows as they danced. Something was moving outside. There was too much movement for it to be a cat or a dog and nominated walker that night. *Nothing ever happens here anymore but you are going to change all of that.*

A fresh rush of adrenaline coursed through him awakening his mind. *Finally after all these years…* He knew – he could feel it in his bones – that the plan was already underway, that the droves of officers were descending on 33 Exeter Street,

Truman Darke trapped inside waiting to meet his fate. He may even be face down on the bloodstained carpet by now, being shackled and dragged away.

The shadows continued to rush past the window, no apparent coherence to the dance they performed for him. He needed to take a closer look.

Laing walked over to the window and threw back the heavy blackout fabric, his eyes struggling to absorb the scene before him.

Shadows were moving, slithering across the ground from all corners, alleyways, drain covers throughout the estate in front of him. The rest of the world seemed silent, asleep and oblivious to it all. Laing stared and marvelled at it. He watched the dark shapes rise from the ground forming thin slivers of ash standing at various heights. The shadows then shifted, morphed and grew in all directions, spawning other parts that resembled gnarly limbs, heavy hands, menacingly long fingers before standing proud with their bulbous, dark heads held high.

Despite their lack of eyes they seemed to stare back at Laing. Uniformly they began to part in the middle, separating to stand in two groups. From between them came the largest figure of all, standing over seven feet tall. As the breeze blew through the avenue Laing noticed the shroud that covered the main figure fluttering in the wind. The face could not be seen from under the heavy black hood but he could just make out two flaming red eyes staring back at him. After exchanging initial welcoming glances at each other the shadows surrounded their leader and sunk to their knees bowing to this man, this creature. The Reaper then bowed his own head towards Laing from the other side of the window.

Father Archibald had been right and the corners of Laing''s mouth curled into a wicked smile.

The feeling of power was immeasurable.

Chapter Thirteen

February 18th 1684

The remaining few hours of the night was interspersed with serious planning and long silences. There was much to discuss but also time required for reflection for each of the three men. Ewan was still feeling the effects of an intense day''s journey back across Wildermoor to the Franklin estate. His back and legs were fraught with pain, for he had not dared stop to rest even for a minute for fear of not being able to find his way back again through the snow-covered clearings.

Edward was torn between elation from having his son back safely and fear for Franklin that he would not survive the strain the search had already put upon him. The mission across the moor would be arduous searching for more obscure clues that may have alrcady bccn snubbed out forever. Edward was concerned for his son also. He could sense that there was something troubling him, and it was rare for Ewan not to share his thoughts with his father. Their relationship had been built on a mutual need for support from one another.

Franklin sat in thought staring into the frantic embers flickering from the fireplace. He could see shadows dancing in the fire. This time he could clearly make out the perfectly angelic face of Evelyn, with her smile that would melt the coldest hearts. She was still out there. He had known it all along. He felt a tightening in his chest spreading down his left arm. He breathed in sharply and silently, and held the breath for a few seconds. After another fleeting shock of pain it passed. He took another sip from his freshly brewed tea savouring the warmth it provided.

Edward decided not to disturb Franklin again and left him to his thoughts as he crossed the room and joined Ewan in the storage room located at the back of the cottage. Ewan was busy loading their packs with provisions – strips of dried meat and bread that would provide them with the strength they would need, canteens of water for hydration and measures of whiskey to take away the pain when they finally managed to rest.

"I don't think Franklin will benefit from any more of that," Edward said signalling towards the whiskey bottle.

Ewan smiled wryly knowing Franklin's demons still haunted him.

"I think we can afford the poor man some respite for what he is about to go through," he told his father.

Sensing again an air of secrecy around Ewan, Edward decided he needed to eke whatever was haunting his son out into the open before embarking on another expedition.

"What are our chances?" he asked, hoping that his directness would win favour.

Ewan stopped pouring the water into the canteens hesitating to answer, the colour suddenly draining from his cheeks. He did not meet his father's gaze.

"I need to know, for all of our sakes," Edward pressed further knowing he was getting closer. "Four days removed from this place does not make a man a good liar."

"I have no idea whom or what we are dealing with," said Ewan finally. "That's what is scaring me."

Edward noticed a tremble in Ewan's voice and for the first time he saw fear in his son. He was fiercely proud of all of his boys but most of all Ewan. He was born into the world a fighter, along with his twin sister Katrina – less than an hour older than him. He never gave in to the same infection that eventually took his mother''s life. But Edward could never understand why Ewan had decided not to fight for his country as his siblings did. He was a home bird and the one Edward could rely on.

Ewan's elder brothers Henry and James had both given their lives in King Charles'' war with Holland during 1672, almost twelve years previous. Grief was what had strengthened the bond between Ewan and his father, as well as Edward and Franklin. The recent years had been solely focused on rebuilding their respective families.

Ewan had always carried a flame for Evelyn. It was no secret. Edward and Franklin had spent many nights in The Weary Traveller planning for the future, for Ewan to come good on the childhood promise he had made Evelyn that one day she would be his wife, uniting the two families, restoring her father's plantation back to its former glory and finally bringing their fortunes together.

It was with heavy heart that Edward listened to his own boy soldier admitting having fear and losing faith.

"Are we in danger?" Edward asked gravely. Ewan solemnly bowed his head.

"Why in God's name do you come back and give the man hope?"

"I wanted to bring him closure, not hope. I didn't think for one moment he would want to risk his own life out there on a whim of one vague sign of her existence."

"The man has nothing left. That girl is his life," Edward saw fit to instil reality back into his son''s thinking. "How did you think he would react?"

"I loved her too, Dad. But after what I have seen I have had to accept that this time our efforts were in vain." It pained Ewan to hear him speak like that. He had kept himself alive out on the plains for days clinging to every shred of hope that he would find Evelyn alive again, much the same as her father did.

Edward one again saw the flicker of sorrow and dread in his son's face.

"What happened out there?" Edward pleaded. "You must tell me."

"That which I cannot explain," Ewan replied cryptically.

"Well you better try, my boy. If you cannot think rationally by yourself, I will have to step in and think for you, to save us all."

Ewan sank into the chair at the small workbench in the storeroom where Franklin used to package up his crops for trips across Wildermoor to the market. It had not been used for months, but still showed evidence of the once rich earth that had helped to build the James Empire all those years ago.

Ewan proceeded to detail his search party's movements, which started four days ago, the night of Evelyn's disappearance. Edward had tasked him to follow the route in which Franklin had heard Evelyn's final screams for help and seen the brief flash of white from her nightgown. They travelled west through the woods that bordered Tewke's Range with the barren stretch of Wildermoor, across the River Wilde at the shallowest point and then after a ten mile trek east they re-joined the trail.

On the second night they found themselves entering the thick growth of the next borderland, the woods which formed the entrance to Harper Falls. Ewan travelled with three other riders, which he had handpicked himself. They had ridden tirelessly to this point, but their steeds could not travel another mile before nightfall, so they set up camp at the riverside to ensure the horses had a steady supply of water.

"I awoke to find it was deep into the night but I could no longer hear the breathing of the others, or the chatter between the horses as they grazed and rested," Ewan recalled. "My eyes would not allow me enough time to even consider my predicament before they closed again. I rose with the dawn's first light, left my horse to rest a little longer and ventured back into the woods. What I found in less than half a mile would change everything and send me back home."

"You didn't find the others?" his father pressed.

"I did…in some respect."

Edward did not need words to encourage Ewan to elaborate. His eyes bore a hole in him hotter than any branding iron.

"I smelt it before I saw it; a smell of rotten brisket, but fresh. It was as if I could feel the moist touch of the blood in the air. As I moved forward it became stronger, but I could not tell the source. Then I heard it, as the ground beneath my boot changed from the crunching of dead leaves to a squelch. I looked down and saw a mass. That's the best way I can describe it. Red with blood, black with dirt from the ground, tinged with pink. I could finally make out shards within it. Torn flesh and shattered bone."

"An animal? A deer maybe falling foul of a flock of buzzards?" Ewan shook his head grimly and continued.

"As unrecognisable as it was, I knew it was human," Ewan said, his voice starting to break as his father watched a tear form and fall onto the bench. "Nothing left but mangled remains of the torso. It was evil, Father. Pure evil."

Edward sat in silence, not wanting to admit that he had no idea how to deal with what he had heard, not bearing to think how Ewan had managed to bottle this up showing no hint of the horrors he had seen.

"How could you possibly tell it was human?"

"Within the mass were shreds of cloth, from a tunic or nightgown. The state of the remains was not the work of man.

The cloth was not from the killer itself. So I ran, for what seemed like hours and miles. I heard a growl from deeper in the forest, which made my heart stop. As I tried to retrace my steps the growl grew louder. I looked behind me, quick enough to see a flash of green followed by another ungodly sound. As I turned to run I tripped, stumbled and fell. I could see nothing, hear nothing but the crack of branches and the scrape of my skin against the rough stones, but I knew I was falling. I awoke in the darkness, I don't know how much later. My head pounded and my body ached. I could feel the trickle of blood underneath my tunic," Ewan said, lifting up his shirt to show his father the evidence; an angry graze on his skin, leading to a large gash across his stomach. The blood had dried but the wound was far from healed.

"Not far from there, there was a glint in amongst the mud and fallen leaves; Evelyn's locket."

"Where?"

Ewan looked up and met his father's eyes at last.

"At the opening to a cave within the forest walls. Or what I thought were the forest walls."

"Where were you? Can you remember what you saw?"

"I don't know. As I looked up, I could barely make out the light shining though the tops of the trees, which appeared as though they stood a few hundred feet tall."

"No tree around here grows that tall, not that is known to any man familiar with Wildermoor at least."

Ewan shook his head in agreement.

"I know where you were," Edward told him. "But it'd be impossible for you to be sitting before me now if that were true. You are describing the bottom of Devil's Pit."

"Devil's Pit?" asked Ewan, "Where is that?"

"You're asking me? You were there yourself!" Edward reasoned.

"I mean why is it called that?"

"The residents of Harper Falls bestowed the name upon it," answered a third voice. Franklin was now standing in the entrance to the storage room having witnessed much of the exchange between the Childs. He was struggling to hold himself together.

Edward and Ewan startled at the sound of his voice, guilty for discussing this behind his back. Neither stood for betrayal, and did not know how to react when feeling accused of it.

"Mr. James, I'm so sorry," Ewan replied offering him his seat and his arms for solace. But Franklin waved him away and walked further into the room.

"Over twenty years ago, Reverend Joseph Yeo lost his position in the clergy by refusing to acknowledge and commit to the new religious regime created by the new Parliament," Franklin continued, "and was exiled for his beliefs. He started conducting secret meetings for worship and blessings hidden from the authorities. The King ordered a reward be paid to anyone who offered up the whereabouts of such rebels and Yeo"s time was running out. One of the villagers reported it but the army could not find Yeo or his followers. After the search had ended Yeo was pronounced dead but that"s when *they* started disappearing."

"Who?" Asked Ewan, looking at his father whose stare was fixed to the floor. He must have known all about this.

"The villagers. The women mostly. The children were next. Nobody knew where they went or who took them but many believed the Puritans were behind it, avenging Yeo's death. There were other reports, however, that more sinister forces were afoot and that the Puritans had summoned evil itself from the Pit."

Franklin walked to the window and stared out at what was left of his land, his mind making the shadows of the past dance again. He could see Evelyn running gaily through the fields, the crops" grown up to her shoulders. He had been stood on the veranda, Christina-Rose next to him, his arm clutching her waist. Now the field was frozen hard from the winter and flat, no green to suggest any life at all.

"All the villagers fled Harper Falls within days and reports are that it has been deserted ever since. Whoever or whatever remains you found, were either one of your party…" he paused steadying himself before continuing, "or my daughter."

"Frank, don't talk like that," Edward asked of him, but he could see that the man in front of him was one who was at the end of his faith, left with little amount of dwindling hope.

"Dawn is here," Franklin said, ignoring the plea. "We must go."

All three rode out of Bradley's Range in silence, as the morning sun began to slowly eat away at the frosted ground.

Chapter Fourteen

She was almost perfect. Her pale white skin smooth as silk and her hair, as black as the night sky, had caught his eye. He had been watching her for a long time thinking that she was The One. He had waited for so long and now she was here.

She was almost perfect, had it not been for the smear of blood that ran from her breast to her slender waistline and stained her perfect frame, a wound across her throat caused by his hand.

William Archibald sighed deeply, pushed his hand against his temples trying to relieve the pressure that had been building up for some time, and sank back into the chair behind him. The chair was hard and offered little in the way of comfort. He afforded himself only the leanest of luxuries in his quarters.

He had already worked for too long tonight and was crying out for sleep, but this was not to be one of his luxuries. It was a burden that he was carrying around, driven on beyond limit by his own obsessive nature. He looked down at the body in front of him. *She had asked for it.* She made him use force on her; she had not wanted to make it easy for him. And after the few minutes of pleasure that he had rewarded himself with her, she spawned an overwhelming emptiness within him, which turned to guilt and then anger. She had forced his hand with the small blade – the letter-opener that he kept in his desk drawer. He told himself that they were all responsible, the five before her too. They were all the same worthless whores but had served their purpose. She was still out there. He knew it.

A knock rapped on his door, which woke him from his reflective state. He beckoned them to enter, and in stepped a hulk of a man, almost seven feet tall and at least half that wide. He answered to the name Stamwell and had been his most trusted advisor for the last fourteen years.

Stamwell entered and took one look at the corpse, then looked up at Archibald. He was not shocked by the sight. There was a silent exchange between the two, in which Stamwell asked simply *another one?* They had an understanding; they would not ask of the others past or motives for the present, they accepted that they were who they were. Stamwell had seen too much over the years for anything Archibald did to ever surprise him. The man-mountain stepped over the corpse to where Archibald sat.

"I'm sorry to, erm, interrupt you, sir," Stamwell started.

"No matter. As you can see I am pretty much done here. This better be worth my time though, Stamwell. I am desperate need of some rest," Archibald replied still pressing his hands to his head.

"The Fielders have returned with another one for you to look at," Stamwell informed him.

"Can it not wait until morning?"

"I think you had better see this one tonight sir. She has had a pretty rough journey and is need of some attention. They are not sure if she will make it through the night, so whatever you need to do, it is advised you act quickly."

A scowl appeared across Archibald's face. He didn't take kindly to being commanded especially by one of his own minions, and he detested sloppy work. The Fielders" only job was to bring the subjects back alive, and in the last few weeks they had barely managed to do that.

Archibald stood up with a sigh of disgust aimed at Stamwell and his incompetent field staff.

"I guess my sleep will have to wait yet again. It appears I must take matters into my own hands. One day I might remember why I employed you lot in the first place."

Archibald walked over to his closet, reached in, brought out his cassock and slid it gracefully over his shoulders. The garment hung loosely on his withering frame, its black fabric swallowing all light within reach. Only the red piping, that signified Archibald's position as Bishop of his chosen flock, shone.

"Take me to her."

"Yes," Stamwell bowed his head and lead him out of the quarters.

*****

She had never considered herself afraid of the dark but that quickly changed. The dark felt like it was touching her, groping every part of her body, but not hurting her. It was toying with her, it seemed.

Evelyn feared what she could not see in the dark but the smell was what hit her first. The dank, dampness of the air and putrid smell of rotten meat stung the back of her throat. She could feel her eyes were stinging and watering too. She could tell she was sat on the ground and could feel the moist earth beneath her and against her cheek. She was slumped against a wall not made of stone but wet earth.

Nor could Evelyn move. She could not feel that she was bound but the pain in all of her limbs and her face had sapped her energy. She felt conscious and nothing else. She was not aware of her surroundings except for the damp earth and had no idea what was going on or why she was there.

She remembered being woken in her bed - what seemed like an age ago - and being dragged away. It all happened so fast that she could not even see her captors, how many of them had taken her or what direction they headed in. She remembered only seeing figures of black, draped from head to toe in the darkness that surrounded her now.

She mustered enough strength to put her hand to her face. It felt clean, free of abrasions, wounds or dressing. She knew she had such wounds elsewhere on her body though, that would justify the pain she was feeling.

She could hardly remember anything, except that she thought she recalled a blow to her head – again it justified the searing headache she was now suffering – and being woken moments before being put into wherever she was now. Her cell.

She felt sick at the thought of what was happening to her. She felt pain in almost every part of her body. Even low down, between her thighs, was painful. That thought alone made her body jolt to meet a dry-retch. Thinking was depleting her energy. But thoughts were something she could not deny herself for the absence of them would be enough to drive her mad.

As she was starting to argue and reason with herself she heard faint footsteps. She could not tell if they were coming from within the same room as her but they grew louder and were drawing closer.

Soon they came to a stop and Evelyn could feel her heart race again, making her chest ache. Her breathing became heavier. She could just make out a faint line of light up ahead, interrupted at certain points. Feet perhaps, or shadows of them.

She could hear whispered voices, and then with a loud screech something appeared before her. She could make out two shapes; one much larger than the other, both as dark as night but bathed in soft light coming from a nearby torch that hovered close to them. Her eyes adjusted but she did not know she was looking at the door to her cell and these were her first visitors.

"Stamwell, shine a light over her. I want to see what we have here," ordered one of the figures.

With that the larger of the shadows grew larger still, the light travelling with him and revealing more of his bulk. He was a massive man with a square jaw, half of his face covered by a flock of hair. She could make out heavy scars on the other half.

Stamwell stood next to her. She could finally see some of her earthen cell. They were in a cavern of some kind. Stamwell shone the torch over her as the smaller figure drew closer. She couldn't see his face well but could see he was a minister of some kind, a member of the clergy. At once, her heart softened slightly as she thought she was saved. *A holy man does nothing but care.*

As she started to believe she would see her family once more, the smaller figure spoke.

"His strength is in his loins and his force is in the naval of his belly," Archibald recited.

"Sir?" Stamwell enquired.

"Leave us!" Archibald hissed at his henchman and for the first time Evelyn could see his eyes, wild and hungry, his mouth pulled to the sides in a sickening and sadistic smile.

Stamwell sighed and reluctantly headed for the door as the light faded from around Evelyn and she descended back into the darkness once more.

Only this time she was not alone.

She could feel his breath getting closer to her. She wondered if somehow he could see in the dark as he found her with no effort. She could feel his skin touch hers, her body convulsed in attempt to repel him; the instinct was to somehow – *any*how - get him away from her.

But it was no use. Her strength was no match for his. Even though the figure he cast in the shadows appeared slender and frail he surprised her with his strength. Evelyn tried to hit out at him but if her hand managed to touch him at all it was with all the weight of a feather in a summer breeze. She heard him snigger as she did so, mocking her as he grabbed her arm and forced it back, putting all of his weight behind it so that within a few moments he had overcome her completely. She was on her back under him on the damp earth.

His hands grabbed and tore at her. She began to shake now as her senses returned. Her body was slowly giving in to the shock. She could not let it for she knew she would not see out the night if she succumbed.

Archibald grabbed hold of her left wrist but was caught off guard when she managed to summon enough strength to flail her other arm at him. He hesitated for a second but long enough for her to reach down into her soul and push all of her remaining strength up into her right arm. Before the demented clergyman could force his weight down even more, her arm flew up and forced her closed fist forward, connecting with Archibald's cheek. She heard a faint crack as her fist made contact. He gasped as the pain took hold.

The surprise of the blow left his body limp for a second and he fell off of Evelyn, flopping onto the ground next to her, for just long enough to allow her to take a few deep breaths. The spinning in her head started to slow as the oxygen returned to her body. However the body next to her was already beginning to stir. Her heart sank knowing that she did not have the strength to capitalise on an attempt to escape.

She could hear him return to his feet, his breathing laboured. She decided that she managed to hurt him more than she initially realised. She may have time yet.

However, the sound that accompanied them in that blind cave chilled her blood and stopped the breath in her throat. It was a sound so guttural; she thought it must have come from the centre of the earth. It had the strength of a thousand cannons sounding at once in a single blast and sounded pained.

It was a cry for help. Then it sounded again, louder, closer. She was breathing so fast that she thought her lungs would shred themselves within her.

The darkness then began to move around her. She feared her head was spinning again. But she had not moved in the last few moments in a way that would injure herself. Yet she could see and feel the room around her move.

She heard a scraping along the dirt walls followed by a sound similar to a roll of wet leather being dragged along a stone floor. A glistening mass was moving. It was not the room moving but something inside it as big as the cell itself.

The scraping continued. She followed the sounds all around her head. Then something moist fell onto her forehead with force, something that stuck to her skin and dried instantly, stretching her flesh in the warmth. That was when she realised it for sure; something was in there with her and the man that had attacked her. Something of such a size she scarcely imagined it was real. It certainly was not human.

The darkness was moving, for sure, but it was made of more than air. It was breathing, growling slowly, plotting. The thing moved quickly and in an instant she felt pain like no other as it took hold of her shoulder.

She could feel the shadows of the beast pressing down on her, her breathing becoming impossible and burning coursing through her body. Her bones started to ache under the pressure until she heard a couple crack. *Her ribs.* The shock of pain left her unable to breathe and something warm build up in her throat, causing her to violently splutter, feeling the liquid from within spill onto her lips. It was warm and salty. Her own blood.

The weight continued to bear down, her body unable to cope with any more. Once more, searing pain gripped her entirely as the feeling of a thousand knives scraped down both sides of her torso. Then she felt a sense of warmth cover her body, trickling down and dripping onto the ground as her skin tore open. The pain started to fade for a moment before returning and shocking her into consciousness so that she could go through it all again. Each time it lasted for fewer seconds.

She was going to die and she knew it.

The knives carried on tearing. Then the weight started crushing her legs, her limbs were moving independent of her body and what was left of her mind as she felt her pelvis being torn open.

Then the darkness took hold again and the pain faded until it existed no more. The consumed her shadows before giving away to a blinding white light.

*****

Archibald exited the cell through the same door he had entered, back into the unlit passageway, feeling his way down the length of the walls. His legs were weak, trembling. In desperation, he tried to breathe deeply enough to replenish his lungs. The corridor seemed to go on forever and soon he grew uncertain he was going the right way.

What possessed him to send away his protector? He truly was going insane. He must be. He had to make his way back to his quarters alone, and fast. His only stroke of luck, as he followed one of the walls that turned a corner to the left, he saw a glimmer of light up ahead, suspended in mid-air. Stamwell was waiting patiently at the entrance to the cavern still holding the flaming torch.

Archibald managed no more than ten paces more before his legs gave out from under him. He groaned with the effort. Stamwell heard the faint cry from further down the tunnel and started towards it knowing there were only three people who stepped foot beyond the cavern door; all of whom meant the world to him. Archibald had provided a home and a family for him as well as an outlet for his anger and lust for brutality. If anything were to happen to him he would become a lost cause once again.

As he drew closer, shining the torch before him to light the way, he saw the figure half-slumped against the earth wall barely propped up with one knee on the ground. He was covered in blood but did not seem to be suffering any wounds himself. He saw the gaunt, drawn face and shock of silver hair and, recognising Archibald, he rushed over to offer his body as a crutch for the old man.

"My God, Father what has happened?" cried Stamwell. It was a rare occasion that he softened enough to show emotion.

"Too much…I've done too much," stammered Archibald, struggling to make any sense. "My abomination..will…kill us all," he continued, in between breaths.

"Don't talk now. Save yourself," ordered Stamwell, picking up the almost-lifeless frame. Stamwell rushed back towards the light that was starting to fall outside of the cavern entrance. The moon stood high and naked in the night sky. As soon as they reached the opening both breathed in the fresh air deeply. It hurt Archibald's lungs but he needed every drop of breath.

Stamwell provided an arm for Archibald to lean on as they crossed the clearing and found another entrance inside the pit walls and descended down into darkness again. Stamwell had catlike eyes; he could navigate his way anywhere throughout the caverns under Devil's Pit and within minutes they were back at the door leading to Archibald's private quarters.

In the light, Archibald could see the mess he had become. His gown was drenched in blood and specked with pink, white and grey; signs of bodily parts and fluids that had been spilled in that room. His stomach contracted and he vomited violently on the floor, disgusted at the state he was in.

"Help me bathe," he told Stamwell, "Get me out of these clothes and help me get clean again. Then leave until I call for you."

Stamwell fulfilled those orders and once the preacher was safely in bed, a night lamp beside him offering a break from the darkness, Stamwell took his leave. He paused at the door and looked back, ashamed at asking.

"Sir, I know I shouldn't, but…the girl?"

"She was The One," smiled Archibald, bringing colour back to his drained face. He looked a different man than the fearful wreck that had been brought back to his room an hour ago. "His very presence there tonight proved it." His sunken eyes glanced up towards his henchman.

"Well done," he congratulated Stamwell. "Is she still alive?" Stamwell asked again, regretting it instantly.

Archibald looked at him with pity, mocking him for his weakness for caring about someone who was merely a subject.

"That would be impossible. I heard her being torn apart before me, in the shadows. She will have served her purpose."

The man-mountain allowed a brief smile to cross his lips before guilt chased it away. "What now?" He asked with remorse in his eyes.

"We wait to be saved," beamed Archibald, "He is finally here."

Chapter Fifteen

Franklin kept a pace in front of the others, as he had done for the previous day's travelling. Edward and Ewan had tried their best to keep up with him but it was evident after they crossed the bordering woods into Harper Falls that he wanted to be left alone. They held their horses back in a gentle trot whilst Franklin cantered on ahead. They both felt they had betrayed his trust back at the cottage and were hoping to make amends along the way.

Franklin needed to be alone. He was trying to prepare himself knowing he was hurtling towards an inevitable truth he could not bear; his daughter was gone.

"We will meet up with him at the riverside," Edward called to his son as their horses strode twenty feet abreast along the woodland track, avoiding the frequent gaps in the road to prevent injuring their steeds.

Ewan nodded but was not optimistic. He had seen a change in Franklin since he had spoken about Devil's Pit. Something else was playing on the old man's mind.

"He knows where we are camping tonight. He won't have the energy to carry on past nightfall, don't worry," Edward continued.

Ewan was still fighting a hidden guilt of his own. He felt as if he had given up on Evelyn whom he loved enough to devote his life to her. Had he given his all in finding her? He was still breathing, which proved he hadn"t.

Franklin opened up an hour's gap ahead of Edward and Ewan and was starting to feel weary. He knew that he wasn"t well enough to be out alone in this place for too much longer. His chest was still riddled with small but suffocating shooting pains, which he had been trying to ignore. He was getting close to the spot agreed by the river where they were going to rest tonight. The same spot that Ewan had found himself a few nights ago.

His horse was losing pace too. Franklin decided it was best for both that they stop away from the track, even for half an hour. He didn't want Edward and Ewan to be alerted to his weakness. At least that way he would still have a lead on them. Franklin turned his horse away from the road and disappeared amongst the army of oak trees. Some of the trees stood skeletal by the side of the road, their leaves not yet returned after a harsh winter. The dead leaves cracked under the hooves. As man and horse disappeared deeper within the forest, signs of the promising spring growth appeared in the heads of the trees that provided a canopy against the world above them. It was still a few hours before nightfall but the light was starting to fail within the woodland retreat.

Franklin's eyes were becoming heavy. His vision became distorted as the effort to hold them open grew too much. But then he saw it; a flash of green. Enough to widen his eyes and refresh his senses like he had slept for days.

He looked around but could see no sign of what had emitted the glow. His horse carried on forward a few more paces and he saw it again out of the very corner of his eye, to the left. He quickly turned his head. Nothing.

Then his horse jolted violently to its side knocking Franklin off and onto the cushion of dried leaves beneath them. Franklin looked up to see the massive frame of his stallion heading down towards him. He threw his body over in a log roll twice and heard the horse's bulk hit the floor with a screeching cry.

Three figures appeared on top of the toppled horse, glowing as green as an emerald fire. Franklin stared in horror as two heads lunged towards the horse's right flank, sank their jaws deep into its flesh and tore away skin, exposing the glistening red muscle beneath. The horse whinnied and screamed and tried to use its strength to roll over onto her injured side in a feeble attempt to crush the scavengers. The third figure stood hunched on all fours looking straight at Franklin. Its body glowed green but it's eyes were burning red, boring a hole through him as it lowered his head readying itself to pounce.

Franklin scrambled to his feet, not taking his eye off the Faerie dog, and struggled to breathe. His legs were lead weights crying out for rest. Franklin turned and did his best to run. As he managed to put together the first couple of strides, he could feel his legs beginning to wake up and managed to pick up pace. He afforded a frenzied look behind him and could see the dog still gaining on him. Franklin ran through the trees looking for any cover he could disappear into but the dog kept coming. It did not seem to experience fatigue and was driven purely by hunger.

A frustrated growl told him that the dog was only ten paces behind. He quickly changed direction and bolted to the left, deeper into another portion of the woods. He hoped that the dog"s night vision was not strong but suspected that with eyes like that they were powerful.

The undergrowth grew thicker now and Franklin could see the green flash was getting smaller. He could afford himself a few moments to try and catch his breath. Franklin let one of the nearby trunks take his weight as he breathed deeper and deeper, taking in all of the air around him. The pain started again in his chest, catching him unaware this time. He clutched at his left arm and groaned. This one was not ceasing as quickly as before.

He stumbled forward knowing he still had to find cover. Then he saw it twenty yards ahead. The trees that supported the canopy ahead and the dried leaves that carpeted the ground stopped dead ahead of him, a vast void lying behind them as if he had reached the edge of the world. *There must be a way around it*, he pleaded with himself and any powers that could hear him, or else he was trapped, providing easy bait for the pursuing Faerie dog.

As he reached the edge and peered over he convinced himself he was done for. There was no way to avoid the fall that lay below. The fifty feet between him and the bottom of the pit would be enough to snatch the life of a much younger man; he may even die before hitting the floor.

As the distant snarls grew louder, he knew the creature would soon be upon him, its blood red eyes fixed solely on tearing his flesh. He had no choice but to try and descend. He noticed to the far right side that the ground fell away in a more gradual decline. Franklin proceeded and tenderly started stepping forward. Agonising seconds passed like hours until he was satisfied that his head was no longer above ground level, meaning it would take the dog longer to find him. Maybe only for a matter of seconds, but they would prove precious to him.

After a few more steps down, the path started dropping away at an alarming rate. Franklin could now clearly see the bottom of the pit but at this height he would still not survive a fall.

Just then he heard a rumble of earth as clumps fell down and scattered on his left shoulder. His heart jumped as he looked up to see the glowing green head above him on the ridge looking straight down with a deadly stare. Franklin's body naturally started to turn and bolt away from the inevitable death he faced and in doing so, his right foot slipped over the edge of the dirt track, giving way to rain-soaked mud, which started to crumble fast underneath the old man's weight.

Franklin flailed his arms, grabbing at anything around him. Nothing offered any support and Franklin's weight pulled his body further over the edge, until his remaining foot had left the ground and he began falling. He fell backwards and immediately felt the claws of the undergrowth slice away his shirt, then at the exposed flesh that came their way. The body of a slimmer, younger tree caught him on the back of the head as the world rushed away above him.

The falling stopped eventually but moments before he hit the ground, Franklin succumbed to the darkness; his right leg bent up to meet his waist, his knee completely shattered. Blood pooled under him as it seeped out through the gash on the back of his head, finding its way out of his body through his ears and nose. His skull had cracked upon impact with the ground.

His lungs tirelessly continued to work and his heart carried on pumping the blood, desperately trying to keep him alive. His body was broken, his mind was possibly already dead but his heart continued to fight even though it was slowly killing him as it did so.

As his life seemed to ebb away, a shadow appeared over his limp body. Franklin managed to muster a final effort and his eyes flickered open. Three hooded figures looked back down at him. Their heads turned and their bodies parted. A monster of a man appeared between them, battle-scarred and bruised from years of tireless loyalty.

One massive hand grabbed hold of Franklin's chest and he was dragged away, into one of the cavern entrances carved into the walls of Devil's Pit, deep down into the earth below.

*****

Ewan and Edward reached the rendezvous by the river but Franklin was nowhere to be seen. Nor was there any evidence that he had been there. No horse tethered to the post, no remains of a campfire. *Surely the poor man could not have survived for these hours without some warmth.*

The night was drawing in, the light disappearing beyond the tops of the trees and soon they would not be able to see their hand in front of their own faces. They needed to press on and hope that Franklin had already made it ahead to the Pit.

They both marched their horses forward for another mile without a hint of Franklin or his steed and were approaching a new disturbing truth; they would have to choose between finding the Pit and Evelyn or launching a new search for her father. The decision was made for them as Ewan spotted Franklin's shoulder pack, hanging like a rag in the sharp thorns ahead. Or what was left of it. Upon inspection Ewan found it had been ravaged; sharp teeth marks had torn the fabric to shreds.

Edward leapt from behind Ewan and grabbed the pack, eyes wide with horror staring at it.

"What animals live in these woods that could have done this?" Edward asked. He had betrayed his friend again by not staying by his side when he was in a vulnerable state. They should never have come out here. He would blame himself forever if he could not find Franklin alive. Both men looked around to try and guess which direction Franklin had gone but they may as well have been looking at the night sky in hope of seeing the sun.

The crushed leaves on the ground provided no footprints either until Ewan spotted a patch of the track, cleared of leaves that lay pushed into a small mound at the base of a tree as if someone or something had travelled at speed, their feet sliding on the wet pile beneath them. It was not much of a sign but it something. They both crept forward and Ewan could see a similar marking in the leaves ten yards ahead, this time on the opposite side of the track suggesting a change of direction.

They followed the cryptic mounds through the thick woodland, eventually being led towards the end of the track as it met a hedge made of thorns. Edward carefully stepped forward to look past the hedge and into the void. The trees ahead swayed lazily in the faint breeze and a glimmer of moonlight seeped through.

"It's here," Edward said looking down finally able to see the floor some fifty feet down.

Edward signalled to Ewan, who peered in the same direction, seeing the familiar void that met the forest floor covered in earth so damp the smell reached his nostrils. They had made it to the Pit but there was no sign of Franklin. They had to descend into its mouth. All they had to do was find a route.

As he turned back around to survey a possible pathway Ewan was met with a blinding flash of light and a moment of searing pain in his temple as the darkness collapsed in around him. His limp body crumpled onto the floor without a sound, as a hooded figure raised his iron club and brought it down onto the back of Edward's head, not giving him time to turn around and notice his fallen son. The blow cracked his skull and penetrated the delicate tissue of his brain with ease, killing him instantly. His dead body turned slightly to the right with the impact, falling onto his back so he looked up at his attackers.

The man-mountain grabbed hold of Edward's coat by the lapels and tossed him back towards the entrance to the thick growth behind them. Immediately a flash of green emerged behind the trees as two Faerie dogs took hold of the corpse by the neck, each pulling in different directions tearing the flesh away, spilling his blood onto the dried carpet of leaves.

Stamwell scooped up Ewan's body and threw him over his shoulder in a fireman's carry descending the path to their left down to the bottom of the pit as the hooded figures followed. They watch Stamwell's massive frame disappear into the cavern entrance and into the shadows once more.

Chapter Sixteen

Archibald had risen from his slumber less than an hour earlier. It had been the most complete night's sleep he'd had in weeks and immediately felt better for it. He swung up to sit on the side of his cot then strained to his feet. Last night he had witnessed their Saviour and a weight was lifted from his shoulders and chest; he felt like he could breathe again.

The years since the local heathens had forced him from his calling as pastor of Wildermoor, he had lived in exile in Harper Falls. He was no longer the man he used to be. In stature he had wasted away, now existing as skin stretched over worn bones. His hair had greyed and thinned within weeks of him being cut off from his people. If he had gone back to the villages he used to serve, he would not be recognised. He had also lost his name and needed to conceal himself from any who may pass through Harper Falls for fear that he would be the Hanging Tree"'s next ornament. As Joseph Yeo, he had held a community in his hands. As William Archibald he lorded over a few faceless figures that had followed him to the solace of Harper Falls, exiled for their belief in the old religion. But now they too were showing signs that they no longer believed in him. He needed to deliver their Saviour to them to restore their faith and finally he had Him, locked in the darkness of a cell deep in the Pit walls. At last they would all be able to rise and take Wildermoor back for themselves.

Still he lacked one piece of the puzzle. The prophecy told of a final sacrifice; an impure life to balance the pure one he had already offered; Evelyn. The Fielders had been dispatched in the early hours to the neighbouring villages back towards Tewke's Range to bring him such a soul. He stood shaking with excitement and anticipation and waited for news.

Archibald had no sooner wrapped himself in the skin tunic, suppressing the little warmth his body retained, when he heard the familiar heavy knock on his chamber door. He held his breath momentarily then summoned the caller.

"Enter," he commanded.

The hulking frame of Stamwell appeared holding his head heavy. Archibald hoped that this was due to fatigue and not the forbearance of dismal news. He stood silent for a few more seconds.

"And?" Archibald snapped irritably.

"Father, we have found them," Stamwell drew out the words as if each one brought him more fear.

"Where?" The Father replied.

"No further than outside our very own walls, Father. Two trespassers were found in the yard," Stamwell referred to the clearing outside the cave entrances. "An old man who looks to have been travelling in this direction, was attacked and fell, followed by a young man who seems to have been travelling a few hours behind him. The old man is barely alive. He must have been unconscious for a matter of hours. He has suffered severe broken bones by the looks of him and the sounds he made when he was dragged down the halls. The young man was apprehended conscious and alive at the time. The old man has been muttering a name – Christina, I believe."

Archibald's eyes widened and his mouth parted at the mention of that name. His breathing grew heavier, his lungs failing to comply.

"Gather the Council at once," the words tumbled from Archibald's mouth before giving way to a brief flash of a smile. Then fear masked his face as it began to turn ashen. "The most impure of souls is amongst us. It is time."

Stamwell looked at the old man with growing concern, not knowing whether or not to follow his orders. His master did not look well. He knew the wrath of the Father was comparable to that of any demon so he immediately took his leave to gather the rest of the hooded figures scattered around the cavern dwelling.

Archibald collapsed back on the bed. His chest tightened. He would rest a while. He needed his strength now more than ever.

They all did.

Chapter Seventeen

Ewan could not decide whether he had opened his eyes or not. The darkness surrounded him and he felt as if he was breathing it in. He could move his arms, and felt his way up his to his face. His fingers recoiled at the feel of the rough, torn skin covering his cheek, covered in dried blood. His head felt like it was going to implode with a pain that swirled around like a cognitive tornado inside his skull.

The effort exhausted him but he tried again to make sense of whether or not he could see. He swore he could hear a rustling in the dark now. He was sitting, he knew that much. He was propped against a wall so damp it felt as if the moisture was eating through his shirt.

He heard the sounds again, only this time heavier, drawing closer but still distant. It drew near until Ewan was sure he could make out the faint rasps of breathing, laboured and ailing. It was slow, each breath drawn in and held for long seconds before a hoarse exhale. The footsteps ceased briefly as Ewan fruitlessly tried to get his bearings. Then a door opened with a creak that startled him. With the creaking of the door came a suggestion of light, which grew stronger until Ewan could make out the rough contours of the inner walls of this place; his cell. The pain in his head lit up again. He closed his eyes until it ceased. When he opened them again he could see shadows dancing on the walls, brought to life by the torch that was carried by a man who led the others, larger than any he had seen before. Even at a distance across the room Ewan could feel his body tense in fear of the figure.

Behind the man-mountain followed six more figures, shadows draped in black hooded gowns. Last to enter the chamber was a man who looked the polar opposite of the group of dark souls; an old man dressed in a robe of shocking white emblazoned with black crosses. Archibald walked up onto a small wooden platform facing the Faceless figures and the man-mountain, and waved towards the giant to close the door. The room was now lit with four other torches around the walls, allowing Ewan's eyes the chance to adjust to the light.

Archibald stood proud at his altar like a king addressing the masses. He carried an air of power and arrogance, holding his head high and soaking in the dank atmosphere around him. As Ewan's eyes scanned the room he saw a wooden table strapped to the earth floor in the centre of the chamber, held by four heavy metal clamps, each roped to the outer chamber walls. Ewan's heart dropped to his knees when he saw the sorry figure that lay atop the table, bound to it by crude leather straps. Lying broken, bleeding and barely breathing, was the body of Franklin James.

*****

"Brothers! Hear me now!" Archibald's voice violently shattered the silence hanging in the air. "The day is finally upon us and we will all be saved!" Archibald stood upon his pulpit, his arms spread wide, addressing his congregation as if he himself were a god. The hooded figures began to show signs of life and Ewan's feeling of terror grew. He was desperately searching the walls around him. He needed to find an escape route. While the figures were distracted, he might be able to slip away unnoticed.

But what about Franklin?

He could not leave him behind to suffer the horrors the demented priest had in store for him. As Ewan glanced down he realised that he could not see his own legs past the knees but there was no sign of blood and he was far from being in pain. He concluded that his legs must have been folded beneath him so that he was kneeling, slumped against the damp wall. He had been locked in this position for so long that his legs had gone numb. He willed his heart to pump the blood harder to his limbs.

Franklin did not move. The only sign that he was alive; his strained breathing. His throat must be injured, thought Ewan. No man could make such strangled sounds without having suffered a trauma.

"I promised you that I would find the Pure One; the one whose innocence would be devoured and brought to life again in each of us," Archibald continued, "and I did. For that subject has now served its purpose and its grace and goodness is now within the body of our saviour."

Ewan became transfixed on Archibald as he spoke. Was he referring to his beloved Evelyn? She was the fairest and purest of creatures Ewan had ever known. The facts were now battling with his hope that she was still alive. But his hope was waning fast. As he pictured her face, his heart could not take the pain of knowing that he had failed her. He had lost her and worst of all he had never told her how he felt.

"And I told you that I would find the Impure One as the prophecy foretold; the one whose soul is black with the tar of sin; the one whose faithless life has been lived only with the intention of bringing down the kingdom of our Lord. Friends, I tell you once more that I have succeeded," Archibald declared triumphantly signalling with his outstretched hand towards the body of Franklin James.

"The people of Wildermoor can keep the Lord they pray to – the very one that we used to turn to ourselves for salvation," he referred to his hooded followers. "We now have our own. And we will sit by his side, for we are the Chosen."

Archibald's gaze did not leave Franklin's body as he spoke. He glided down from his pulpit through the six hooded figures waiting, hanging on his every word, and into the centre of the room to where Franklin's crumpled body lay.

Then almost inaudibly, as if he were talking to himself, Archibald muttered,

"The one who thought he could bring me down, taking away my very essence of being." The priest bent down beside Franklin so his mouth was close to the old man's ear. "I told you I would be back, James. I warned you that I would take everything." Standing back up and addressing his congregation once more, he roared "And now I offer that to our saviour, for my work here is done!" Archibald turned quickly to meet Stamwell and barked another order at his giant henchman. "Summon the dungeon guards! It's His time now."

Stamwell left the chamber, his torch lighting the hallway dimly as he made his way deeper into the cavern. He could just about live with removing the dead bodies of young women whose capture he had overseen, and convinced himself that it was all for the Father's own sexual gratification. But he had seen a change in him. The warm arm that had taken Stamwell in all those years ago had turned to a cold embrace that was threatening to take Stamwell to the same depths of insanity as Archibald.

He had watched Archibald become obsessed with redemption, finding their true saviour and raising him to restore order. For years he had raved about finding this figure and he now believed he had.

Stamwell had only seen the creature once. Archibald had spent a week locked away in the confines of the cavern Stamwell now found himself walking towards. When he had returned to his living quarters, Archibald had not spoken for another week. His fixed stare and pale skin scared Stamwell, for only the second time in his life.

Archibald had then started sending Stamwell and the Fielders out at least once a week to scour the nearby villages, to find more *subjects*. He had resembled a man who had worked out the equation to the meaning of life but who still had to rely on trial and error to obtain the final figure, a man trying to find something but would never say what.

Then one night he had finally broken down in his quarters in front of Stamwell who had been shocked to see Archibald in such a state. The priest had been inconsolable as he raved about damnation and demons coming to claim his soul. For a man of faith, it had been disturbing to hear him talk of such things.

"Do you fear anything at all?" Archibald had asked Stamwell, catching him off-guard. Stamwell had not known whether Archibald was genuinely interested in his answer or accusing him of being void of fear.

"I fear for you now, Father," he had responded, "I have never seen you like this."

Appreciating the concern, Archibald had raised a wry smile.

"I am doomed," he had said. "My soul is not long of this world."

Stamwell had refused to let Archibald condemn himself and kept trying to reason that he was sick, perhaps delirious or delusional. Archibald's façade had hardened once more with Stamwell's insistence as he tried to convince him that his sanity was still intact.

"I will show you if I must."

"You do not have to show me anything to prove yourself to me, Father. I owe you my life and if you say you are okay then I shall lend my peace to this matter and it will be forgotten."

Archibald had been on the brink of agreeing and brushing everything under the sheepskin rug that lay on the cold stone floor in his chambers. But he had known he could not. The little humanity he still possessed would not allow him to do this to Stamwell. He insisted once more he show him the truth.

With that, Stamwell had followed Archibald through the dark, dank corridors deeper into the caves. At the end of the final long passageway there had been a large oak door with a heavy knocker and a sliding viewing panel from the inside. It was the door Stamwell now stood at, once again.

With the same trepidation that he felt on his first visit, he pulled the heavy steel knocker back and let it bang against the door twice, echoing up the corridors and out into the night air. Stamwell waited until the viewing panel was noisily pulled back and revealed a pair of narrow, suspicious eyes. The eyes said nothing but acknowledged Stamwell's presence with a widening stare.

"Is he ready?" Stamwell asked.

The eyes grunted in response and then disappeared behind the viewing panel once more. Stamwell heard the heavy bolt and within seconds the door was opened to reveal another dimly lit cell, the largest within the network of tunnels, and Stamwell slowly entered.

As Stamwell stood and searched the darkness, his eyes slowly adjusted to make out a glint of light running some ten feet down the wall. The flicker of the lit torches illuminated two chains that ran parallel, ten feet apart. Both were met at the top by a shelf of glistening skin. The chains shook violently every few seconds, met with a menacing and chilling growl, almost resembling breathing. Stamwell's gaze continued up until he met the two red orbs hovering in the darkness.

The eyes were set deep inside a massive head covered in wet, scaly skin.

"I pray thee won"t judge me. One day I hope to explain to you the reasons why I have done this." The words replayed in Stamwell's

mind from that first night he had been allowed into this chamber. Archibald had behaved like a shamed father desperately trying not to lose the loyalty of a son.

Before him stood a creature, twenty feet tall. At first it resembled a man until Stamwell registered it was supported by legs of a goat, the size of oak tree trunks. Its hooves sunk into the damp earth under the weight of its massive frame. Hanging down behind it was a tail; Stamwell could not tell its full size but could hear it scrape against the wall behind. Its face was fierce, it's skin pulled tight over a massive skull, and two horns grew out of the forehead, as big as those of a mountain bull, tapered to tips sharpened to provide a fatal blow. He had never felt his body numb like this before. He had the urge to vomit but each of his vital organs had seized up in the creature's presence.

Its mouth opened, as if surveying Stamwell's frame for size, and he saw the teeth. His mouth was filled with hundreds, thousands, of razors that would break through bone as if it were sand.

Stamwell heard the shadows of Archibald's voice once again. "I have been chosen. *We* have been chosen to receive our saviour at last." The Reverend drew in his breath through his teeth as he prepared to name his creation.

"Apollyon. The angel of the bottomless pit. The Lord's destroyer."

*****

Apollyon stared down at Stamwell again; the movement of the monster's mouth made him feel like he was being measured up as its next meal. But Stamwell felt stronger this time, more in control of his fear of the creature.

"What does he want us to do with him, then?" One of the dungeon guards slurred.

Stamwell felt like he was awoken from a state of trance himself. Those eyes had a way of getting hold of you but Stamwell did not feel overcome by the beast, unlike Archibald.

"He has summoned him," replied Stamwell managing to draw his eyes away from the creature. "He is ready to conduct the Ascension Rite," he referred to the ritual of redemption and salvation that Archibald had told him about that first night here.

"Where?" the guard asked dumbly with a gratuitous grunt.

"Where do you think? He has convened the Council in the Arterial Chamber. He is to be taken there at once," he spat the last word and headed towards the door.

"You're not going to help us then, cocker? Expect us to manhandle this thing all on our own?" exclaimed another guard.

"You'll be fine," he lied.

Stamwell opened the door and quickly made his escape, letting it slam shut again behind him. He rushed back towards the Arterial Chamber, pausing once or twice to catch his breath. His heart was pounding too fast now for him to keep up the pace.

He couldn't watch this man fall deeper into insanity or whatever he had created. He decided to follow orders no more, for his heart could no longer bear the pain of losing another father. His shoulders were not broad enough to carry any more guilt and for the first time in his life he knew that there was nothing he could do.

Stamwell stared at the doors in the hope that divine voice would instruct him. But he knew he had to act on his own. Stamwell walked past the door to the chamber, his guilt mounting and heart breaking with each step. He kept ascending the corridors of the caverns, further into the darkness, searching for the light of the moon and did not look back.

*****

Archibald waited nervously within his congregation, the set of black-hooded faces staring back at him expectantly. He was beyond nervous. He feared once more for his life, for he had made too many promises to the Council to try and convince them of his worth and legitimacy. Too often he had failed them.

Ewan had given up struggling in his shackles. As he moved, more blood flowed back into his legs and as the feeling came back so did the pain. His eyes rarely left Franklin, whose minimal movements were starting to wane. He was watching a man he considered his second father slowly pass away and was powerless to stop it.

His thoughts were disturbed when he heard a faint rumbling, muffled through the thick dirt walls. It was intermittent to start with but grew louder and more persistent. His breath stopped in his throat when he heard the first roar bellow along the corridor outside. Whatever it was, it was drawing closer. He felt his body grow cold. That roar was inhuman. The echo resonated through the walls and he could feel short, sharp tremors in the ground beneath him. Accompanying the cry was a faint jingle, which created a harmless symphony.

Ewan felt his legs start to wake up underneath him, causing more discomfort. It was as though they were trying to carry him out of this place on their own accord. His flight response was kicking in. Once again he knew he and Franklin were in danger and these figures in the room meant them mortal harm.

Ewan was startled by three slow, deliberate thuds on the door. Archibald also appeared surprised at the sound. Archibald composed himself quickly and bellowed his customary command to the caller,

"Enter."

The door slowly opened and the two dungeon guards entered, each trailing ten-foot of heavy wrought iron chains, the links of which were an inch thick and five inches in diameter. As the chains followed behind them, the massive, hulking frame of Apollyon was led, doubled over in order to fit through the door.

Some of the Council staggered back a few paces, hands on their chest in exclamation but the hoods disguised if it was surprise, joy or horror. As Apollyon cleared the doorway, he raised himself to full height. The ceiling in the chamber was almost as high as ground level. All the members of the Council were now huddled against the far wall opposite to where Apollyon stood.

Twenty-feet tall, his tree-trunk legs pushing his gargantuan torso higher, his massive head now surveyed the ceiling above him. He opened his mouth and bared his teeth, running his tongue across them in an almost-human but sadistic grin.

As the Council watched in bewilderment, Apollyon took two huge steps towards them. They huddled closer and scrambled further down the rear wall of the chamber, reaching out to grab each other for security. Their faceless, menacing stares crumbled within seconds.

"Behold….Apollyon. The Angel of the bottomless pit, the saviour of the faithful and the Reaper of The Damned!" Archibald said with gusto, standing in front of Apollyon as the monster's gaze fixed on him. "Release the chains," he commanded the dungeon guards, "and leave us." They hastily wrestled with the locks on the chains at Apollyon's wrists. As soon as the locks freed and the chains dropped to the ground they turned and disappeared from sight.

"My Lord," Archibald addressed the beast, "Our gift to you." He spoke softly to Apollyon, and led him with an outstretched hand to the centre of the room, and the table on which Franklin lay.

Ewan couldn"t watch. As soon as he heard Archibald mutter those words he had to succumb to his own weaknesses; he was powerless to stop anything happening to the old man now.

Apollyon's eyes widened as he looked down at Franklin, his head tracing the length of his body up and down. He looked from Archibald and back at the body several times, asking for permission and encouragement. Only when Apollyon's stare was fixed onto Franklin once more - and Archibald's presence no longer provided a distraction - did the priest take his leave from the circle. He backed slowly away from the beast, the one that he himself had raised, towards the remaining figures of the Council and stood triumphantly before them.

Ewan continued to look at the terror that was taking place before him, too entranced to turn away. He was pleading inside for Franklin to rise up from the table and run… and keep running until he was far away from the madness. But it was no use. Tears started to well and sting in Ewan's eyes. He had failed them all; he had failed the three who he loved the most, and had even led two of them to death.

Apollyon's mouth was parted in a permanent grin, sneering at the form before him. The chamber was filled with bated breath. Apollyon finally lowered his head towards Franklin, his eyes still investigating the length of his body. The beast's head now rested inches from Franklin's bruised and bloodied face. Its jaws widened even further causing the serpent-like tongue to fall free of its cage slapping Franklin's face with a moist touch. He dragged the tongue over the surface of his face, covering it all in thick gluey saliva. Ewan watched in horror as the massive jaws came down and parted either side of Franklin's head. Franklin's body now appeared as one with the beast.

Ewan saw Apollyon's jaw-bones tighten. He looked away in horror, squeezing his eyes shut in an attempt to wake up from the nightmare unfolding before him. But his ears did not fail him. He heard the crack and snap, joined by the muffled cries as the beast squeezed down and crushed Franklin's head as easily as biting through a rotten apple.

Archibald clasped his hands together and rubbed them satisfactorily, marvelling at the beast's display of hunger and power. Apollyon savoured the bite, sinking his teeth lower into Franklin's flesh, slowly turning his bones to splinters. His head finally lifted, and with it Franklin's face slid away from his skull. His blood now pumped freshly and freely into a pool, beneath what was left of his head, gently trickling onto the earthen floor. The flesh that had once made up his gentle mask now hung like a scrap of meat from Apollyon's jaws.

Ewan's hands briefly fell from his eyes and he froze when he beheld the ghastly sight. He felt a rising in his throat and turned his head to vomit. His head hurt as it tried to make sense of the chaos.

Apollyon looked down at the remains of his first meal, the head drenched in fresh blood. He bowed his head once more and lapped up as much as he could with his tongue before opening his jaws wide again and sinking his teeth into both sides of the torso, tightened his grip once more and violently shaking his head, tearing open Franklin's chest. The skin and muscle tore away just as easily and the beast devoured it in one gluttonous mouthful.

Archibald stood in awe of the monster he had raised himself. He had finally acquired the power he needed to prove his worth to the Council and to save his eternal soul. He glanced back to the cowering hooded figures as one of them drew closer to him, entranced. Archibald tried to muster words of warning, but his breath stood still in his throat. The figure continued towards the beast. It stood no taller than Apollyon's thigh and when it was within touching distance, it extended a hand towards his leg.

The Council member's hand touched the hard, scaly flesh. The other hand reached up to the hood and slowly pulled it down. There stood a woman, pale-skinned, dark hair flowing down her neck and tucked into her hooded gown. Her head rose up towards Apollyon, her mouth parting into a smile before opening as if a laugh was about to escape. At the touch, Apollyon's head snapped over his right shoulder and looked down at her. He scowled, his brow furrowed into an almost-human expression of anger. The woman's hand shot back from his skin. Archibald could hear her struggle for breath as she looked up at the monster. For the first time, Archibald felt cold blood course through him. He had raised the beast but at once realised that he had no idea how to control it.

Archibald silently prayed. Not to the demon before him but to the God he had betrayed. In that moment he started to feel regret. He had not gained power but had instead unleashed it in its most destructive form.

Apollyon's body turned fully to meet the woman's fragile frame as she continued to back away. She had no time to run or turn from him as Apollyon's right hand reached out and grabbed her, picking her off the ground like a feather and pulling her closer to him. Within seconds his jaws were wrapped around her neck and with a single gentle sweep of the head, her throat was torn open. Her body convulsed as her breath spluttered out through the wound.

"No, no….no, NOOOOOO" Archibald screamed clawing at his head.

Apollyon threw her body to the ground with a sickening crunch as her neck and back broke. Tears streamed down Archibald's cheeks as her body lay in a crumpled, bloody heap before him. He looked up at Apollyon, weeping and praying for mercy from his own creation.

The beast continued forward towards Archibald, whose body was trembling uncontrollably. Another hooded member of the Council launched forward towards Apollyon. The figure got within arm's reach of the creature, before Apollyon batted it away with his left arm. The body left the ground and clattered against one of the chamber walls with a soft thud; the sound of another cracking bone as the limp body crumpled onto the floor. This drew Apollyon's gaze from Archibald for precious seconds, long enough for the priest to get message to his legs to leave.

As Archibald ran for the chamber door, he met the eye of a man across the sacrificial floor; the other prisoner who sat chained but struggling to make his own escape. Ewan wrestled with the shackles binding his legs to the wall and was frantically trying to dig away the dirt from around the base they were attached to. The dirt clung under his nails and softened his grip, making him work harder with each handful he managed to grab, until soon he started to feel weary again, fatigue returning to his arms and legs.

Archibald started to open the chamber door but a foreign feeling stopped him from going through. Guilt was holding him back; remorse was compelling him to help the young man who had borne witness to the horror he had directed. At his age he probably would not get very far alone anyway. A young, strong set of hands was what he needed.

For the first time since the beginning of the ritual, Archibald thought of Stamwell. He searched for the massive frame that had followed him for years and had served as his own shadow.

For the first time in all those years, he was not by his side. And for the first time since he could remember, Archibald felt alone. He needed the prisoner, whoever he was. He was his only hope. In order to leave his sins in the caves, he needed to seek redemption.

He saw Apollyon surveying the carnage at his feet and knew he did not have long before the beast focussed on him again. The beast knew not loyalty to he who created him, only pain and destruction. Archibald tried to run over to Ewan but his legs were made of rubber. Ewan struggled with his chains, his arms feeling like lead pipes before finally he conceded defeat and slumped back against the damp wall. He had given up hope of finding Evelyn the minute he awoke in that place and he had seen Franklin's fate. Now he was giving up on himself. His only hope was that his father was safe, perhaps on his way back to Katrina at The Weary Traveller, already planning another rescue mission.

He was dumbfounded to see the demented priest hobbling towards him, with his hands outstretched. The old man looked pleadingly towards Ewan, spending his last breath to make it across the clearing to him.

"I can help you," Archibald cried breathlessly, then edged closer, "but you have to help me too".

Ewan looked at him blankly; the confusion and amazement left him speechless. Moments ago he had summoned the Antichrist and now he was trying to make a deal to save them both! Ewan's head dropped in a vacant nod. Archibald stumbled over to where Ewan was slumped and fumbled in the pocket of his gown.

Despite their trembling, Archibald's hands finally found the keys. He could hear Apollyon's grunts behind him becoming angry and impatient.

Ewan's own hands were struggling to keep still as he watched the old man wrestle with the key chain, and he breathed a brief sigh of relief when he saw the single silver key emerge from the priest's garment. He waited for what felt like eternity with his hands out before him until the click as the key sank into the lock, followed by the drop of the shackles from his wrists. Ewan momentarily wept, but as quickly as the emotion had risen within him, it was sucked back deep inside as he witnessed a horror take place inches from his own eyes.

For a moment he thought he was blinded. The artery was sliced by the beast's blade-like claws. Archibald's face remained frozen against the torrent that spewed from the opening in his throat. The sounds he heard as he struggled to wipe the blood from his face told him there was nothing he could do for the old man. He was forced to listen to him die.

Ewan finally regained his sight, the chamber still nothing but a blur. He could just make out the hulking, grotesque shape of Apollyon ten feet in front of him hunched but still towering over the limp, shredded body of its creator. Apollyon's body remained still, giving a sense of purpose to its thrashing arms as it cut away Archibald's flesh. Whimpers were heard amongst the ungodly growls and grunts, weakening after each strike until the body eventually gave up the fight. Ribbons of flesh hung down from Apollyon's claws like trophies from each kill.

His limbs slowly began to jerk back to life, as his brain urged every inch of his terrified frame to move. As his senses started to return, he retched when he finally breathed, smelling and tasting the foul air that started to fill the chamber. The odour, the sounds and the images of this hell started to overcome him once more. The air was tainted with the copper-essence of spilled blood, and the visceral remains of the Council met each glance as he turned his head.

He spied the way out - the *only* way out – an impossible hundred yards ahead; the door the guards had clambered through, when they had made their swift exit, remained open. More fortunate members of the Council must have been able to take their leave whilst the beast and Archibald had been otherwise engaged.

He turned once more towards Apollyon, who still busied himself picking the remains of the scattered bodies beneath him. He estimated that he could make it if his legs still possessed the speed and strength they once had which seemed unlikely. Still he hoped.

Ewan's body was acting on instinct and made the decision for him. He scrambled to his feet and briskly took two paces. Apollyon remained undeterred so Ewan tried a run. The pain shot up through his feet, his knees and up the centre of his back stopping him momentarily, as his body fought to keep itself moving.

That moment cost him dearly. The soft crunch of hardened dirt beneath his feet as his body stopped dead instantly alerted the beast. The massive head shot around as if released by a catapult, its red eyes fixed on Ewan as a mixture of blood, drool and grey matter oozed from the corner of his mouth. The snarl that followed emanated from somewhere so deep within its stomach, that Ewan wondered if it were from the ground itself.

Ewan took two more steps.

He heard and felt the mammoth frame shift and lurch towards him.

He managed three more steps before the ground was taken from under him, and then returned to him with a force that brought the darkness back to envelope him. But this time it was not warm and comforting.

All light faded as consciousness left him.

The ringing inside his head brought Ewan back to consciousness, but only briefly. His eyes were still blurred; the pain in his head quickly spread through his entire body. His eyes managed to focus long enough to make out the massive bulk of Apollyon, above him. As his eyes became heavier he thought he saw not one but two shapes above him, the second appearing just as large as the beast, shrouded in black. The end was near and now all he could do was pray it would come swiftly.

Chapter Eighteen

March 10th 2002

Truman awoke to find the room still in darkness. Not that he had slept much. His body was stiffening more every morning. The mattress on the floor had worn thin, the duvet having also seen better days. It did little to keep the chill away, though spring was finally on its way.

These days, he found it difficult to bring himself to close his eyes. The drink helped in a way but the more his mind relaxed around his constant nightmares the less his body was fit to fight off sleep.

She came to him at night, mostly. The image of Lorraine Thacker stayed with him throughout the day too but at night he could almost reach out and touch her again, talk to her, tell her he was sorry and that he…loved her? Would anything have been any different if he had actually forgotten his pride and bravado for once and actually told her that? Probably not, knowing how stubborn she could be. But it may have meant his warnings about Colin Dexler would have held more weight. Truman may have even done more to help Lorraine, and to stop her getting so close to that monster.

Dexler was a monster, an animal. Truman had experienced every emotion imaginable when Commissioner Roberts had marched into the Criminal Investigations

Department on that day two weeks ago. There had been a call, he said, from a frantic patient at Wildermoor Brook. Two bodies, he had been told. The news had caused mini explosions in Truman's mind, then had come the A-bomb that would kill all hope, joy and faith that Truman had clung to throughout his life. One of the bodies was that of Lorraine Thacker.

After those words were uttered, silence descended over his world. He did not hear any more that Commissioner Roberts said. Even the level of noise in the rest of the department, which at times drove Truman to insanity, faded away. He felt as though he was falling to the ground. They could not identify the second body as the face was damaged beyond recognition. Truman later heard from a few gossip agents that there was suspicion, according to the Commissioner, it might have been Lorraine's receptionist, as she had gone missing shortly after lunchtime and never returned to her desk.

Truman vaguely remembered being escorted from the offices and out onto the street, his mind still numb until the confusion set in. Whatever had gone on between him and Commissioner Roberts in that office still remained a mystery. He understood he had to be kept off the investigation due to his past relationship with Lorraine, but to be deemed unfit to fulfil his duties was a kick in the teeth.

Then he had committed a fatal error. His judgement had been clouded by rage and grief. Later that night he had found himself at Dexler's front door, trying to break it down with his fists. He had known Dexler was there. Where else would a man like him go? But there had been no answer. No curtains had twitched suggesting he was inside, cowering from Truman like he expected he would. Truman had told himself to leave, that this man simply wasn't worth it and that it would not be long before his men would find Dexler and put him inside to rot his final days in Wildermoor Prison. He would be miles away from anyone or anywhere that he could cause any more harm. Except to himself. But Truman welcomed that thought.

As he had started to walk away, his eyes had spied an alleyway he had failed to notice before. No longer in control, Truman had made his way down to the broken garden gate at the end of the walkway. A few paces into the garden, with a helping hand from a few discarded plastic crates lying against the garden fence, and Truman had been in Dexler's back yard. The back door had been unlocked and too tempting to resist.

Stop. It could be a trap. Truman had chosen to ignore his common sense once more. Years of lawful intelligence had faded in one moment of madness as he had marched through the door and into Dexler's kitchen-diner. Nothing had seemed out of place, except for the cold, stale air that hung in the lifeless room. Truman made his way through the next open doorway and into the hall. He had felt no remorse when he had found the cold, dead body of Dexler slumped against the front door. Someone had gotten to him first.

No sooner had he knelt beside the corpse and felt for a pulse on the chubby neck, before the striking on the door and the shouted orders came from outside. They had come for Dexler finally! But why had they been shouting Truman's name instead? How had they known he was there?

He had had no time to ponder the question. His escape had been swift and messy, out of the open back door, scrambling over the next three neighbouring fences and away into the night, away from the flashing blue lights that had shone down the length of Exeter Street.

But now, without Lorraine he had nothing to live for and without his badge he had nothing left to lose. Whenever he pictured Dexler's face, he saw Lorraine's. When he saw hers he could not bear to close his eyes again. So he reached for the half-empty bottle beside the makeshift bed and took a large gulp enjoying the warmth it brought. The taste was stale. He had neither the inclination nor the strength to leave the solace of the room he had acquired for less than the price of a decent meal. He had not ventured far enough to find fresh water to rehydrate himself, not even to brush his teeth and have a shower, for about three days.

His mouth was dry, his face thick with bristles and his body stained with dry sweat. To let himself fade away in this hell-hole would have been a betrayal – to those he had inspired on the force, to himself and most of all to Lorraine.

He needed a wash. He thirsted for a drink that would invigorate his senses rather than mute them. He yearned for somebody to talk to, to help, to unload the thoughts that plagued his days. Most of all, he desperately needed to know the truth of why this had happened to him. He was determined to find out.

As he began to rouse himself from his bed, his head dizzying with vertigo, an envelope slid under the door of his room. The only person who knew he was here, to his knowledge, was the landlady, who worked nights down the main stretch of Harper's Hill, and to whom he had not divulged his real name. So how the hell could he have post, especially at this hour?

He picked up the envelope and rang a finger along the seal tearing it open. The effort made his fingers hurt, as did all of his joints. So many sleepless nights and forgotten amounts of booze must be reducing his immune system. He was also succumbing to a cold.

As he took out the slip of paper – the size of a compliment slip you"d usually expect to find included with a free pen - from under the seal, his heart paused for the time it took him to take in the elaborate scripture written on the page.

Someone had just read his mind.

*****

I know who you really are. Let me help you. Time is running out.

The envelope was not addressed to him, or anyone in particular, and the plea written on the blank slip of paper was vague in its intentions. Stapled to it was a business card – simple black text on an ivory background, the symbol of triangle playing-card spade in the top right-hand corner, the only insignia. It may have been intended for one of the other residents of the hostel but he didn't believe in coincidences.

Something inside him stirred. He had been trained and had trained others to be suspicious of everything until they were able to prove there was no threat or malice intended. *Guilty until proven innocent.* But he had the overwhelming feeling of hope, something he had not felt for many weeks, perhaps even months. He inspected the back of the slip and the card for any more evidence.

The address was printed in miniscule text in the bottom left-hand corner of the card. He was drawn to the name in bold above. He could not place where he had come across it before but the name seemed familiar. An old comrade on the force? A drinking buddy from his training days? He drew a blank. How about the less favourable of his past acquaintances? A defence councillor, a crooked judge or slippery criminal he had helped entrap in order to get the sorry son-of-a-bitch behind bars?

The name of the practice manager, Dr. Mason Stamford did not mean anything to him. No, it was the symbol on the card that was calling him.

*****

Truman found the psychiatrist's surgery easier than he expected. He had not been to this side of Wildermoor since he was a teenager. In those days he and his small band of mates would cycle from the centre of the barren moor, through the forest across to the remains of Harper Falls, a place that one would never think could once have had inhabitants. The tracks that had been roads were now so hidden beneath fallen leaves and years of mud-slides and the trees so overgrown that the only remaining evidence of the village were lumps of hard stone. The forest had claimed Harper Falls and had choked its life away with relentless bracken tentacles.

The forest opened on the other side to a recent development, known as Shepherd's Beach, named not for its proximity to the sea (the nearest shore line was at least eighty miles to the north and a hundred to the west) but for the retreat it had offered those who had once worked the harsh, unproductive fields across the face of Wildermoor.

Truman eventually found a small building. The only indication that he was at the right place was a small gold-plated plaque displayed next to the front door, underneath the door-bell.

The door was open and inside Truman was met by a friendly receptionist; a rarity in normal NHS doctor's surgery's these days. The service was a lot more punctual too; he only had to wait a few minutes more than his allotted appointment.

After receiving the mysterious card and note under his door, Truman had sworn he would take no notice of it. It must be a hoax or scare tactic. He knew that the police team he had raised were instructed to find him or were waiting for him to wander back into the town as though nothing had happened.

Two more double-measures had calmed his nerves that night and had sent him back to sleep. It was then that he saw her face yet again. Only this time Lorraine seemed to be trying to tell him something, her voice so faint that he could not make out a sound. Her eyes and hands pleaded and he cried in his dream. He wanted to help but felt he was failing her, just as he had in the last hours of her life.

Behind the shimmering image of the woman he once loved, more and more shapes began to appear, some shrouded in light and some as black as night. The light from the others –

the desperate, pleading souls – began to fade in the presence of the shadows, as though their very existence was being sucked into a vortex.

Truman could have taken this as some sign from a divine authority but it just confirmed to him more that he needed help. Maybe he needed something to help him sleep, or maybe he should give up the drink. Whatever it was, something was not right with him. Maybe the anonymous note and invitation had been fate's way of telling him to get his head sorted out.

The man who appeared from within the office surprised Truman. He was not what he had expected. Dr. Stamford stood no more than five-foot-five; smart cropped black hair peppered with grey flecks, dressed casually in a Nordic-patterned sweater and dark jeans. The oddest thing about him was what he wore on his face. He had expected the thin-framed spectacles – it was a pre-requisite for medical practitioners to wear them these days, it seemed – but there was something different; he wore a smile. Not a creepy, forced, I-must-look-happy-for-my-patients smile, but one that was warm, welcoming, comforting and, above all, content.

Truman instantly felt at ease with this man, and felt that he had known him for years. The doctor had yet to speak to him but he already had the urge to open up and tell him everything. Coming from years of erecting a barrier between himself and society - all in the best interest of his career and himself - teaching himself to be wary and suspicious of everyone he met, Truman found the feeling unsettling.

"Mr Lockwood?" Dr. Stamford stood in the doorway, smiling. Truman recognised the alias he had adopted since fleeing Wildermoor. He stood up, now feeling apprehensive and regretting agreeing to come. He wasn't yet ready to have his head split open and his emotions dissected on the slab.

Dr. Stamford offered his hand and Truman shook it, once again putting him at ease. His legs stopped trembling.

"It's lovely to meet you," Dr Stamford said warmly. "Thank you so much for agreeing to attend. Please come in," he stepped aside and invited Truman into his office.

"My pleasure, Doc," Truman replied through gritted teeth.

As the door closed behind them, Truman immediately felt trapped. The doctor''s office was smaller than expected. The wooden-panelled walls darkened the room but at the same time gave a homely feel to the place. Despite its less-than-airy nature, the room exuded safety, comfort and seclusion from the outside world. Just what people need when they spend an hour of their time – and more of their money – delving deep into their psyche. This was officially the last place that Truman ever expected he would turn.

Mason Stamford made his way over to the sideboard at the far right of his office, where he was busying himself with the caffetiere.

"Could I get you a coffee, Mr Lockwood, before we begin?"

Truman was lost in thought, scanning the room with an inspector's eye. Impressed with the number of frames and recognition plaques that lined the wall behind the desk, he could see that the man was certainly well-qualified.

"No, no, thank you," stammered Truman when the doctor glanced over his shoulder to prompt him. "If you don't mind, I would just like to get down to business. Why is it that I am here?"

Dr. Stamford, with his coffee mug in hand, walked over to the chair on the near-side of his desk and stirred his drink through. He seemed mildly amused by the question.

"You're asking *me* why *you're* here? That statement alone gives me the impression that you are a lost man, Mr. Lockwood, but - correct me if I''m wrong - it was you who booked your appointment, was it not? Please, take a seat," he motioned towards the comfy couch opposite the slightly more modest office chair in which he positioned himself.

"Indeed I did," Truman was embarrassed by his clumsy statement, "but only in response to an anonymous, not to mention mysterious, invitation to come here." Truman sat on the edge of the couch and leaned closer towards Stamford, resting his elbows on his knees. "Correct me if *I'm* wrong but I can only imagine that came from you, Doctor."

Stamford pondered the comment before answering carefully.

"You are, of course, correct, Mr. Lockwood."

"Please, call me Ash," Truman wanted to make the experience a little less formal and to make himself more comfortable.

"OK…Ash, you know this can be a funny business. You see just about every kind of person walk through those doors, recognise their problems in an instant and never get to know the *real* them. If I passed half my patients on the street, I would not know them from Adam or Eve. I spend the whole time examining the inner workings of their mind and I never get the chance to take in what the person is really all about." Stamford took the chance to lean in towards Truman and spoke in a whisper.

"I have to say that I'm not sure I follow. What does this have to do with me or the note you sent me?"

The doctor sat back in his chair, sighing as he reclined. "In most of my cases, it takes me a long time, many sessions, to scratch the surface with my patients, before I discover the real reason why they have come to see me."

"I'm sure the fees they pay for the privilege softens the blow." It was Truman's turn to try and break the ice with humour. Stamford was not so amused.

"But with you, Mr Lockwood, I had you figured out before you even came here, before you even knew about this place." Stamford smiled, displaying pleasure as he spoke. "Hell, I would even wager that I know more about you than you do."

Truman stared into the eyes of the doctor as he spoke. The warm demeanour that he sensed the moment he first saw Stamford began to wane as he wondered whether the doctor had all his own screws tightened.

"I doubt that very much."

Stamford's stare was strangely hypnotic and Truman found himself feeling as though he had floated away from his body. He did not enjoy the sensation that he was not in control of the situation he volunteered himself into.

"We have never met and I have only been in these parts for a matter of days. There's no way you could know even the simplest things about me. I'm sorry to disappoint you, doctor."

"Again you are correct – about some things, at least. Yes, you have only been in these parts for days and no, we have not met whilst you have been here. But that does not mean I do not know you, and that we have not met before…" Stamford spoke with conviction, the tone of his voice becoming grave, "…Mr. Darke."

Truman's breath caught in his chest as once again he was caught in Stamford's stare. His eyes had grown cold; his face appeared more ashen and had lost the glow that once made him appear so alive. Without blinking or shifting his gaze from Truman's own horrified face, Stamford muttered breathlessly.

"Have you ever considered regression, Mr. Darke?"

Truman was right, this man was not all there and the situation was not all it seemed. When he entered the seemingly serene office, he had clung to the hope that he could use this time to relieve some tension, even release some of the guilt, which he carried since he fled the town. He felt as though he was frozen to his seat with an invisible force pressing him down. He could feel the weight on his shoulders as he watched Dr. Stamford rise from his chair and glide effortlessly towards a locked cabinet on the wall next to his desk. He keyed in a simple three-digit number and removed a black leather pouch.

The syringe he held was small, but the needle attached to it almost doubled its length. It couldn't have held more than one millilitre of clear fluid, Truman estimated. The substance had already been drawn back before it was placed into the pouch. Stamford had planned for this – whatever *this* was – before Truman's arrival. Maybe even before Truman had even picked up the phone to make the appointment that morning. It had not occurred to him it was odd that he had been able to get a slot to meet with the doctor so quickly.

He had been trapped – tricked – for the second time in as many weeks. Only this time he had brought it on himself.

"What the hell-", whispered Truman, as he watched Stamford raise the syringe to the light. Appearing satisfied, he turned back to face Truman, holding the syringe in a way that Truman held his own cigarettes – which he was now yearning once again; *just one drag, just to calm my nerves and stop my hands and knees shaking.*

"You seem tense all of a sudden, Mr. Darke," Stamford declared showing no concern. "I told you I am here to help you, only if you will let me."

"What sort of help is *this*?" Truman signalled to the syringe Stamford held. "Who the hell are you?"

"Who are any of us?" The doctor questioned. "You are not who you said you were when you entered my office, you are not even the person you think you are and I may not be the person you think I am. It's a puzzle, wouldn't you say?"

Truman had no idea what Stamford was talking about. Everything about this meeting was becoming more confusing and surreal with each second, and now he was questioning his own sanity more than ever. He knew he had to leave the office, leave the building and get as far away from this man as he could. Truman had spent an entire career dealing with citizens who were unhinged but this was the first time he felt scared to the point he himself had felt threatened. He lacked the backup and support of the Wildermoor Police force but decided to use the best bluff he had to bide him some time.

"You stay away from me, Stamford. I can have my guys here before you know it."

Stamford scoffed.

"Your *guys*?! You mean the band of miscreants that run this godforsaken town, who you devoted your life to bringing up as your own? The very same that turned on you at the first whiff of your guilt?"

Truman stared at Stamford for a few seconds longer, his brow creasing into a deep frown as his eyes fell towards the floor.

"Don't think I don't know what happened to you back there, Truman," he said, using his Christian name for the first time. "Didn't you wonder how there were so many of your men surrounding Dexler's place so soon after you arrived?"

Truman started shaking his head, not wanting to hear it. What made it worse was that this man – as deranged as he was – still made sense. Yes, the same questions had crossed his mind on his journey across Wildermoor that night, but he refused to believe it could be true.

"I thought that they had gotten a lead on Dexler, linking him to Lorraine's murder, or had followed mine. We had a trace on him for weeks."

Stamford couldn't tell whether the broken man was talking to himself or whether he was trying to convince himself he had not sealed his own fate back at the house in Exeter Street. In truth, Truman was no closer to answering that question either.

"There was no lead! No trace," mocked Stamford, "You were the only one chasing that guy. And since we are on the subject, did you not think to question how – *why*? – you were called here today?! My God, man, you are pathetic! You're blind and we all see you for what you really are." The words carried barbs that cut deep into Truman's flesh.

"Some divine purpose, perhaps?" Stamford teased, reading Truman's thoughts once more. "A higher power that was sending you a sign? Again, you're right about one thing, there is a higher power, a ruler and creator of all, but believe me when I tell you that he is not smiling on you," Stamford snarled, drool escaping the corners of his mouth as he spat his words at Truman.

Truman needed to call on the last ounce of inner-strength he had, to leave this place as he had left behind his old life. He could escape Wildermoor completely. The whole place was turning on him, pointing crooked and condemning fingers at him. He rose to his feet, without looking Stamford in the eye.

"I'm leaving," he declared as he made for the door.

"I wouldn't recommend that." The doctor's initial poise, sophistication and warmth returned to his voice, and the man that had just berated him returned to its shell. "There is a small matter of my fee," Stamford said with a smile. The mask of the madman had dropped in a second and Stamford appeared once more the ever-caring health worker.

The blood started to course through Truman's body once more, his heart pumping like a piston regenerating every organ and fibre it could. Truman slowly straightened and turned back to face Stamford. The pleasant and expectant smirk written on the man's face made his blood boil.

The next few moments passed by in a flash. The space between the two men seemed to evaporate and Truman was on the doctor before he had a chance to realise or mount any defence. The single strike of Truman's fist caught Stamford squarely across the jaw and floored him instantly. The blow had not knocked him unconscious but left his body motionless on the floor. After a couple of tense moments – in which Truman feared he had killed the man – Stamford started to stir. Truman wanted to strike him again and rain down his fists not giving him a chance to look up. He wanted to stomp him into the ground until he was one with the concrete below.

He brought his fist down across Stamford''s cheek. *This is for me.*

Another struck the back of his head as the doctor tried in vain to protect himself. *This is for Lorraine.*

Truman raised his arm for one final blow. *This is for Evelyn —*

Wait.

Who's Evelyn?

And why did Truman have the sudden urge to avenge her, to make this man pay for whatever hurt he had caused her? Truman now began to believe that he was slowly losing the few marbles he had left. He looked down at the crumpled, groaning frame of the doctor; the man who had introduced himself as someone who could help less than ten minutes earlier. *What have I done?* The blood from the cut that had opened across Stamford''s scalp now coated Truman''s clenched, bruising fist.

He remained looking down at Stamford, both of them struggling to catch their breath. The doctor was face down on the floor in front of his desk but was starting to force his frame up. Truman took slow backwards steps towards the door.

As he grabbed the handle and pulled the door wide open, a flash of white appeared in front of his eyes and a searing pain travelled through his head. One blow was enough to knock Truman to the floor. It all happened too fast for Truman to see the man behind the fist that hit him. All he saw was a mass of black – the man was huge, must have been dressed in a dark robe from neck to toe with a mass of black hair, or maybe a hood, covering his head. He lay motionless on the floor, temporarily dazed by the fall. The heavy kick that connected with his ribcage brought him rushing back to consciousness, the air escaping his lungs again before he had a chance to draw any back

in. He heard a crunch, followed by a shock of pain as one of his ribs broke. His head was spinning and he could not focus. Even his hearing was disorientated and he heard a wall of confused noise and illegible ramblings somewhere behind him. *That must be Stamford*, who had finally come to struggling with his speech due to the swelling that had already set in under his cheek. His jaw had also been bruised but it did not seem to tame his ravings.

"Get him," Truman could hear him groan at the massive assailant now in the room, as he struggled with his words. "…Couch."

The man's strength was unparalleled. Truman was suddenly floating up from the floor and within seconds was on his back on the sofa. Lying on the couch Truman started to wonder whether Stamford actually had any other patients.

But Stamford"s client base was not Truman"s main concern. All he could think about was the pain in his head, the broken rib and the confusion at how he had ended up in there in the first place. He was struggling to breathe, due to both the pain and the pressure that was being applied to his shoulders and throat by the boulder-like mitts that held him down. He could not move. His eyes finally began to focus once more, as they darted from left to right trying to get his bearings.

Stamford stood at the small, waist-height table underneath the cabinet that he had unlocked earlier; his frame was now slightly hunched as he fought to keep his head up. His head was still spinning from the force of Truman's attack and the shock was slowing him down.

"Hold him!" The doctor barked at his assistant. Truman felt the man's hands tighten their grip on him pressing down harder onto his shoulders, making Truman wince and groan as the fingers dug into his collar bone.

Stamford appeared above Truman again brandishing the syringe. This time, however, there was no stopping it. No wise crack remark or loaded fist could break Truman out of the vice-grip he was being held in. Truman's left arm was forcibly twisted around, baring his forearm to the air. The sting that followed told Truman the needle had found its home in one of his veins.

The warmth spread through him in seconds, causing his muscles to sag and relent, followed by the slowing of his breathing and heart rate. The room stopped spinning and every object around him became an incoherent shape, blobs of colour until the darkness started to creep in.

"Goodbye, Mr Lockwood," he heard Stamford say. "Goodbye, Mr. Darke," the voice was becoming distant.

"Goodbye…" The voice called him by a different name, one he could not make out, as the darkness and silence took their unshakeable hold.

*****

The body lay motionless on the couch. Stamford's own, leaning against the small side table behind him for support. Breathing deeply, he was finally starting to regroup his thoughts, not once moving his eyes from Truman's limp body. The man's eyes were closed and he looked anything but peaceful. His right harm hung towards the floor, his mouth open but his body was as taut as it had been when he was feebly trying to fend off Jeremiah Grayson.

Grayson and Stamford had worked closely for the last year. The huge man was considered the Council's smoking gun; with a seemingly immovable frame that towered close to seven-feet tall and weighed almost three hundred pounds. Some members of the council had voiced their distaste at their newest acquisition, believing he was nothing more than hired muscle. In this situation though, he proved to be exactly what Stamford had needed.

"Clear up this mess," Stamford addressed Grayson breathlessly. "We need to move out."

Grayson nodded with a grunt and carefully shifted Truman's body from the room. Stamford never ceased to be amazed by the giant's agility and attention to detail in his work. Whenever he was called to conceal evidence of the orders he was forced to follow, he ensured that the task was completed swiftly and with no fresh damage to the subject. In short, he handled Truman like a baby, cradling his legs with one hand whilst supporting his head and shoulders with the other. The dead weight was not an issue for Grayson, another reason why he was so invaluable to the Council's cause; feats of inhuman strength were often called upon.

Stamford stopped Grayson as he got to the door to provide him with another order.

"In the boot of the car," he said and was once again met with a satisfied grunt and nod of the head. Once the big man had carried his quarrel from the room, Stamford surveyed the office. It had been a fine creation and the performance had been pulled off without a hitch. Well, maybe one small one, he thought, as he brought his hand up to gently massage his jaw. A little bruising and stiffness for a few days was nothing when suffered for the right cause.

The doctor quickly swept around the wall behind his desk and removed the frames that held his medical qualifications – images copied from an online search engine, blown up to A4 size and framed. They provided the ultimate prop that had fooled the stupid police officer. Although Truman had not been just a police officer, Stamford knew that as did the entire Council. How he could not wait to return to Blacktor Hall with his latest prize; The One who had eluded them for so long.

Gloria, the plain, dowdy woman who had posed as the surgery's receptionist to greet Truman, returned to Stamford's side as he packed all of the frames back into the cardboard box under his desk. She had removed her hair from a bun so that it cascaded down to her shoulders, changing her appearance dramatically and took ten years off her. She was, of course, only twenty-eight years old but had been one of Stamford''s lovers since the day she had turned eighteen. She had been the most loyal, asked the fewest questions and had never minded aiding her man in what he referred to as "housekeeping" for the council; essentially all of the hard work that the higher powers could not – *would* not – dirty their hands with. Gloria stood close to him, right hand on her hip, making her left hip curve out from her body. Stamford looked at her realising he wanted her there and then. Adrenaline always brought about a power trip in him that could only ever be satisfied and manifested physically with Gloria. *Not now, not here. There is too much to do.*

The office remained perfectly as they found it. The annexe they had rented remained still and silent, as it would have been when used as a residency years before. It once belonged to the family-run undertakers next door, which had been forced to fold the previous summer.

"What now?" Gloria asked sweetly gazing into Stamford"s cold eyes with her own.

"We make it look like we were never here."

Her lips quivered as he spoke to her and held her stare. She reached in as his face moved closer and caught her lips in a deep embrace. Heavy footsteps stopped at the door signalling that Grayson had performed his last task promptly.

The trio left the office and hurried through what had been the reception area. Gloria climbed into the back of the waiting black Mercedes while Grayson held the door for her.

Stamford was the last to leave, closing the door behind him but not bothering to lock it. They hadn't bothered acquiring the keys to the building; they had never needed to. He paused briefly as he started down the short, grass-lined path towards the car, and then turned to walk back towards the door. He removed a small multi-tool device from his pocket, selected a small crosshead screwdriver and used it to remove the four screws from the plaque hanging below the doorbell. *No evidence, no trace* – that's the only rule they had set him. He had always prided himself in his immaculate work ethic.

Leave no trace, they had said. In whatever way he wanted to take care of Truman Darke, had been left that up to him to decide.

Chapter Nineteen

The darkness eventually gave way to a searing light. At first it appeared as a small speck in the distance that grew as it loomed nearer. It soon gathered the pace of a runaway train, until the entirety of Truman's peripheral vision was encased in a sheet of white. His eyes squinted against the glare, waiting for the moment to pass until he was once again able to open them. The moment never came but his eyes opened anyway and seemed to adjust to the sudden change in surroundings.

Truman stood in the centre of a huge room coated in the clearest of white. The walls stretched so far beyond a point that he was unable to comprehend where they met and formed corners. A white universe surrounded him; a place with no true end and of no obvious beginning; no limits yet no horizon. Soon enough, he could make out a shade of gold, growing in size as it drew near. It appeared to float of its own accord until it was close enough that Truman could make out two sparkling blue spheres – *eyes* under the wave of gold – *hair* and a pale but warm shade of tan pink. A face; one that Truman felt he knew. It was the most beautiful woman he had ever seen wearing a gown of pure white. Her slender hands were the only sign of a worldly body beneath the garment. She floated effortlessly towards him.

Since waking in this room, Truman was aware that despite

being totally naked (which in itself was a cause for concern for he never possessed the confidence for such a state) he was warm. There existed no breeze and no apparent source of heat, but he was content. Nor did he feel any pain, despite the constant aches that had possessed him for the last two weeks, not to mention the fresh wounds and broken rib from the beating he had sustained before the darkness arrived. In fact, old scars, one on his cheek from an over-zealous knife-wielder and an appendectomy just below his stomach, had disappeared. His skin was smooth and unblemished, his face cleanly-shaven, his head clear and his eyes and mind open wide.

Something had happened to him after the incident in Dr. Stamford's office and he was beyond trying to make sense of it.

The figure came within a few feet of him and he felt something new for the first time since arriving here. He could feel his heart pounding hard, as if it wanted to break through the casing of his ribs and jump into the arms of this woman.

He knew her. There was no mistaking that. The emotions that were coursing through his body were ones he had felt before but had failed to convey when he had the chance. He wanted to weep at the sight of this woman. In life – which he was beginning to believe *this* was not – he had masked these feelings, had wandered or stumbled through the years behind a barrier. But who was he protecting? Himself? How could denying love be good for any man?

The woman stopped walking, floating with only a foot between her and Truman. The smile gaped on his face and tears welled up in his eyes. They failed to drop from their ducts. It seemed that no emotion, fears or pains could materialise. In that room, at least.

He wanted to reach out and take her in his arms. *Just one last time.*

"Hello Truman," the velvety voice spoke.

"Lorraine…" It was all Truman could muster before he fell to his knees.

Truman's worst fear was confirmed with the sight of Lorraine. He knew now that he was no longer alive. How could he be? How could the image of Lorraine be so real this time? He could reach out and touch her, feel her touch *him*, be able to smell her hair and feel her breath. Was this a dream? Yes, she had visited him before in his state of slumber back in his flea-bitten, rented bedsit but he always knew that it was his mind that had conjured her. Standing in front of him, he knew now that she was as real as she could be.

"Lorraine, I..." his voice trailed off for a moment as he tried to gather his thoughts. "I'm so sorry, I should...I didn't...I should have been there, I should have stopped him, or stopped you from-"

"No, Truman," she said softly, cutting him short as his voice started to break. She could see he was trembling. She crouched down elegantly and put her hand on his. It was warm as he knew it would be. "I was not yours to save."

"You were," he said on the verge of tears that would not come. The words felt as if they were choking him.

She smiled and gently shook her head. It was her way of telling him he was wrong but that it was okay. Still holding his hand she drew him back up to his feet.

"I was hurt when you said that you couldn't help me, yes, but not for long. I knew you, Truman. You were only doing what was best for me and deep down what was best for you too."

He shook his head harshly, his way of telling her now that she was wrong. But her smile somehow made it all seem ok, as if it was all meant to have happened this way.

"But your purpose was not to save me. You have a much higher purpose than that, and I know that now. I have seen it."

"Seen what?" He was bemused

"Your future," she informed him, "Your purpose. Your destiny."

"This is insane." Truman could not – *would* not – believe that he of all people had any kind of higher purpose. His life had been largely lived within a sea of discontentment and misjudgements. He was not the material for any kind of divinity.

"Is it? Does any of this make sense right now?"

She motioned her hands across the expanse of white light around them. He shook his head again. His mind felt serene as well as being on the verge of breaking down. So much so that he felt as if he was going – or had already gone – completely mad. This place was beyond comprehension for any sane mind. He started to believe that he was beyond saving.

"There are things you need to see," she continued, "to prepare you."

"For what exactly?"

"For what you must do and the people you must face. You need to be prepared."

"I have no idea what you are talking about," he protested. "For all I know I am laying in another drunken stupor born out of another night's self-pity,"

He immediately regretted spoiling what should have been the perfect reunion with the only woman he had ever loved.

"Then let me show you," she stepped forward and wrapping her arms around his neck, pressed her body tightly against his. He closed his eyes, soaking in every second of the embrace, wanting this moment to last forever.

The light rushed away and the darkness returned. This time the dark brought with it new colour and a place he had once known.

Chapter Twenty

The sun broke through the canopy of the trees overhead, chasing the remnant of the cool night air away, making way for another day. The flecks of warmth soothed his cheek as he slowly started to regain consciousness. His ears absorbed every sound around him; every flutter of the leaves in the gentle breeze, the distant birdcall welcoming the sunrise and the howl from a dog hidden away amongst the trees. His nostrils flared as he drew in his first deep breath and the smell of damp mould with it. The smell was much too close.

The skin on his left cheek, unlike his right, felt taut. It too told him that the ground was sodden and cold. March evenings were still chilly. The effort it took to slowly raise his head from the forest ground surprised him. He was not prepared for how little strength he appeared to have left in his body. His head sank back down and became one again with the dank ground. His eyes grew heavy as he struggled to resist the allure of sleep. He had no idea how long he had slept for already and why it had done nothing to rejuvenate his senses. He had no idea where he was. *Too many questions for this time of the day. Just let me sleep some more.*

The sudden rustle of dry leaves, from a spot dried by the morning sun, startled him so that his eyes opened almost as soon as they had closed. Relieved, he realised that he was not alone.

The footsteps grew closer, muted along the way by the carpet of wet leaves. Whoever they belonged was no small man. *That"s if they belong to a man at all*, a thought that started Truman"s heart thumping harder. He was in no fit state to fend off any kind of attack or predatory intention. Instinctively, his hand bunched into a fist in readiness, clasping a thick clump of mud as it did so.

A huge foot stopped a few inches from his face, causing his hand to loosen its grip on the forest floor. A mud-ball was not going to help against anyone this big and monstrous.

A large paw grabbed his shoulder and gave a gentle shrug. Then a deep, gruff voice spoke down from above.

"I didn't think you were going to make it."

Thanks for the reassurance. He had not yet regained enough strength or awareness to determine whether he was awake, dreaming, alive or dead. Was that really something he had to decide for himself? Right now? Couldn"t someone just give him a sign instead?

The boot rose slightly and leapt towards Truman, connecting with his upper shoulder and forcing him onto his back. A shock of pain rushed across from his shoulder to his wrist. *Yep, that'll do it.* Apparently you can't feel pain in dreams so this had to be real.

Excess clumps of dried mud fell from Truman's cheek and brushed his mouth as he drew in as much air as he could. The air tasted fresh, even though his mouth felt stale. He gazed up towards the ceiling of green and welcomed the spots of yellow sun that broke through.

"Here," the voice said again, bring Truman's attention back to the man-mountain stood over to him, a hand reaching down towards him as the figure stooped down lower on his trunk-like legs and presented him with a bunch of bright red berries. "It's not much," he continued regretfully, "but it should see us through the first day."

Truman looked up at his face, confused. Stamwell saw the man's brow crease.

"Who…," Truman managed to force from between his dried lips, "Where…" he added craning his head up in an attempt to survey his surroundings.

"We have time to talk," Stamwell said, "but now, you must eat." He offered his open hand once more. "We must move before the sun is too high. We must move with the shadows whilst we can."

Silently, Truman accepted the fruit. The taste was sharp and sour, but the rush of saliva in his mouth felt good. Greedily he devoured the rest of the bunch before looking guiltily up at the man who had helped him.

"Don't worry," Stamwell reassured him, "I ate before plotting out our best path."

There was a silence as Truman sat up, wincing at the pain that woke in all of his joints. His head pounded as he struggled with a momentary bout of vertigo. Stamwell helped him to his feet, taking the burden of most of Truman's weight. *This would be a long journey*, he realised. He had allowed four days, hoping that this man would last the distance and that they would get enough of a head start. They would surely be tracked and followed as soon as the light allowed it

Stamwell was not sure that the beast was dead and did not want to take any chances. Gathering the battered hessian sack that hung loosely from the nearest elm tree, Stamwell carried Truman as they both hobbled into the safety of the trees, escaping the emergent daylight.

The first hour passed in silence. Fatigue was partly to blame, as the men battled the trek with their own physical wounds. The mental scars that they had suffered formed a casing over their minds, protecting them from any sights and sounds that projected through the forest but the images of what they had both witnessed played over and over again behind their eyes, offering no means of escape.

The cover of the trees stretching for miles, their entire horizon a blanket of greens, browns and a shade of deathly-black.

The further they walked, Truman regained the strength in his legs and his back straightened enough to be able to support his weight again. His face still bore the brunt of the blows he had sustained. The mud remained caked on his left cheek but protected the deep cut that had sliced through his flesh. Even now he was not aware of the extent of his injury or what had caused it. He just knew that it hurt. Not searing, as it had been the first time he had tried to move and touch the affected parts of his body, but now its entirety throbbed in a single dull ache.

He had no idea who the big man was as he followed; another moment of instinctual trust when he had not asked any questions. He did not know the man's motives, but could *feel* his good intentions.

Truman felt unease flood over him, a sudden sense of dread and he could not explain why. With every step he was trying to piece together *why* he was *where* he was. He tried to think of home; of somewhere he last felt safe. And of someone he had loved and who had loved him.

His mind was blank. Not because he had never felt safe or loved, but because his memories were fading. The man he was – everything he used to be – was disappearing.

As if on cue, Stamwell spoke.

"What is your name?"

Truman stopped dead in his tracks, thinking the question over more times than he should have needed to. He was being tested; that was why he was here, this man had been sent to help him discover himself.

Darkness still shrouded Truman's mind blocking his thoughts. Slowly, sullenly he answered.

"I only wish I knew."

With a touch from the man-mountain's hand on his shoulder the world around him rushed away. He watched as the trees surrounding him, the ground beneath him and the sky above him disappeared into an all-consuming void. At the end of the void shone a light so bright, he could see it although it was many miles away. The light rushed towards him until once again he was back in the room of white.

Chapter Twenty-One

This time he knew to open his eyes straight away and that no discomfort would come from the glare. Once more, his pain ceased to exist and warmth bathed his naked body. His mind was busy trying to decipher the pictures he had just seen, just felt. *He had been there, hadn"t he?* This question remained unanswered as once more, upon the effervescent horizon, he watched a figure approach with the same effortlessness with which Lorraine had moved.

This time it felt different again. Without seeing any features, face or hearing a voice, he already knew this person. Once again it was a woman. But this time it was *the* woman; the one that he had spent his entire existence looking for.

He could feel it rise from the pit of his stomach as she approached. His feet no longer felt as though they were touching the warm, pulsating floor. For the first time since waking up in the white room, his body felt alive – not just content, relaxed and serene but actually *alive*. He felt the blood rushing through his veins. He felt in tune with every single atom in the universe and the feeling only grew stronger as she drew closer.

Her night-black hair swayed as she walked, just as it always had. When he finally saw her face, he was relieved to find that she still had the dimples in her cheeks when she smiled. She was in every way as perfect as she had ever been. Her skin was pure and blossom white, just as it was the last time he had seen her.

Long ago. *So long ago.*

She did not have to speak before he knew it was her.

"Evelyn," Truman said breathlessly, a smile never leaving his face. His eyes started to sting again for the absence of tears.

She returned his smile sweetly.

"Hello Ewan," she purred, "I've been waiting so long for you to find me."

Chapter Twenty-Two

March 10th 1684

Stamwell stirred constantly throughout the night and woke the next morning with a fever. The crisp white sheets clung to him through the sweat that had seeped from his relentlessness. The throbbing in his head was affecting his sight. The four days and nights spent in the forest, tracing and re-tracing their steps to try and find their way out of the trees and towards the safety of home, had taken its toll.

The wound across his shoulder had re-opened again during his fitful sleep. Every night since they had reached Tewke's Range three nights earlier, he had woken to find the sheet beneath him blood-stained. The wound must be causing his fever; an infection was surely setting in. The skin was raging hot and painful to the touch. He must make the journey into town to see the doctor or ask Ewan to call him to the house. He sat up in bed making the same promise he made each morning. He knew he would not follow it through. He had never had the need for doctors in the past. Father Archibald had always been able to provide the care that Stamwell needed, which was never often. Archibald had often remarked at Stamwell's strength physically, inside and out.

As he sat on the bed, goose bumps running over his arms and chest responding to the chilled air hitting his clammy flesh, he looked over to see that she was still there. Her perfect body, turned away from him as she slept on her side, but still there for him to marvel at unashamedly. She was the most perfect creature he had ever seen.

Ewan was not entirely pleased with the courting that had occurred between his twin sister and Stamwell after the first night of their return, but he could see that in one day Stamwell had made Katrina happier than she had been in her twenty-one years prior. He also owed the man his life so had no option but to give his blessing.

Katrina was not like most other women. She possessed a man's mind, owing to the years that she had been raised under the protection of her father, three brothers and every other father in the village. She had been brought up as a fighter and a grafter. In the absence of Ewan and their father, she had taken the reins of both Tewke's Range and The Weary Traveller, ready for the men to take over once more upon their return.

Katrina and Ewan often shared the same thoughts. She had prayed for her brother and father each night they were away. However, one night she had awoken knowing that only one of them was going to return. At sunrise, she had sent two of the farmhands from Tewke's Range into the forest to help bring them home. Later that night, she had run into Ewan's arms as he had entered The Weary Traveller at last, his body visibly broken and shaken. With him he had brought another man, who emitted the air of a protector. Her first contact with Stamwell had been a gentle touch to one of his thick arms and a kiss on his cheek as she had whispered a heartfelt, "Thank you."

It had been the first moment that she had felt the surge of electricity from a man, a spark. There was something else about him that had drawn Katrina to him. She felt safe with him. Growing up, she had always felt shielded around the village as every man and watched out for her, and their sons longed to be with her. But standing in front of Stamwell, she had barely noticed there was anyone else around.

Likewise, Stamwell had felt lost within her green eyes. She possessed a child-like innocence that he wanted to protect, but such a womanly presence that he wanted to gather her up in his arms and disappear to anywhere that they could be alone. Her green eyes, her auburn hair, the curves of her perfect body; he wanted her then, all for himself. Stamwell realised then that there were emotions that he had never felt whilst living within the confines of the Council.

Whenever she laughed it pulled at his heart. He had spent that night by her side watching her drink ale by the pint with the regulars who were all celebrating Ewan's return, whilst also toasting the memory of their lost friend, Katrina and Ewan's father, Edward. When she had cried for her father Stamwell had cradled her in his arms, racked with guilt at being the one who had caused her pain, recalling how he had fed his body to the demonic pack of dogs. Stamwell had been thankful that at the end of the night, he did not have to say goodbye to Katrina. He returned home to Tewke's Range with his hand in hers and that is how they stayed.

After learning of the death of their father, Ewan had taken over as the head of Tewke's Range in honour of Franklin and Evelyn James and took his responsibility for Katrina's safety as seriously as their father had. In Stamwell he saw someone he knew would protect and take care of her. They had been inseparable since they had met, but Stamwell still found time to tend to the remnants of the James family land. He rose at dawn and was next seen at sundown heading to the Weary Traveller with Katrina in tow, where they would take up residence in the shaded far corner of the inn, cosy next to the roaring open fire.

It was an idyll that Stamwell had never experienced or dreamed of. Although he had served Archibald loyally for years – since owing his life to the priest – he had never known that kind of life existed. He had been promised power and domination. The start of his new life at Tewke's Range had shown him how wrong his old master had been, that his kind of power was not what every man craved. He hated Archibald for it before he started missing him again. He had been close to the Father for many years and the feelings he once held were hard to forget.

The wound throbbed enough for Stamwell to take in a sharp breath, waking Katrina, who jumped at the sound. She turned over onto her right side to find him grasping his shoulder.

She trailed her slender finger across his back to comfort him. Silently, she was letting him know she was there. He flashed a flicker of a smile. A sign of their infatuation with each other was their ability to communicate their love without words. Stamwell then rose from the bed and disappeared beyond the cover from the stone wall, into the adjoining bathroom.

The faint moonlight from outside that softly illuminated the bedroom and the outline of Katrina's perfect form, filtered through around the corner of the wall reflecting off the bathroom mirror.

Stamwell, as he did every morning, stood and stared into the mirror taking stock of the blemishes brought from a lifetime of toil and sacrifice. The new wound glistened like the inky surface of the ocean at midnight. One swipe of Apollyon's claws had opened up the skin on his shoulder stretching down to his chest. The blood shone black in the moonlight. The wound appeared to pulsate, opening and closing with every beat of his heart. *Just an illusion. It must be the light playing tricks on me in the mirror.* He clasped his right hand once more over the open wound attempting to hold the skin closed. As the pressure lifted, albeit it for a moment, his mind flickered back to his last night in the cave.

After leading the beast to the sacrificial chamber, the massive, snarling, hungry stare and growl of Apollyon bearing down on him, making his bones feel as if they were shrinking. Upon his initial escape, Stamwell had reached the mouth of the cave before an invisible force had stopped him and forced him to go back down into the depths, where the horrific unveiling was still taking place. He could not abandon Father Archibald, the man who had saved him from abandonment and rejection all those years ago. Despite all of his wrongdoings, that man had never betrayed him. He may have been too late but he could not bring himself to leave the cave without trying.

On his route to the sacrificial chamber, Stamwell had detoured to Archibald's private quarters, where he knew a concealed weapon had been hidden in the back of his wardrobe since the day they had all moved underground, away from the prying villagers of Harper Falls.

He found it shining in the darkness. A two-foot blade on a gold shaft, the sword was heavy. Stamwell had been the only one down there who had demonstrated that he could handle such a weapon, and Archibald had said he would bestow the sword on him when he was in a position to assume power. Stamwell decided for himself, and on Archibald's behalf, that now was that time. He had to find the power to stop the abomination that had been created.

Upon returning to the chamber, Stamwell could not have prepared for the scene that lay before him. Battered, broken and shredded bodies strewn across the floor, all members of the Council. He could tell that there were fewer bodies than had descended the caverns earlier that night. Some of them must have been fortunate enough to get away. The beast was twenty feet away, distracted by a fleeing prisoner – one of the men that Stamwell had brought down there himself – when Stamwell noticed the motionless body that lay close to his right. The garment, previously a brilliant white surrounded with exquisite red stitching, now lay on the ground, covered in sprays of thick, dark blood. He could also see a shock of white hair protruding from beneath the remains of the cassock's hood.

Stamwell knew who the body belonged to but he had to see it for himself. With one hand he managed to turn the lifeless body over onto his back.

The white hair and chosen garment, or remains of it, were enough to convince him that this was William Archibald. The flesh from his face was hanging loose and the muscles beneath were torn beyond recognition.

The rage that he had been trained to subdue for so long, the very same short fuse of emotions that Archibald had wanted to harbour in order to assist with his future domination, had rushed to the fore. Stamwell gave a wounded cry just as Apollyon slammed down the body of the prisoner effortlessly to the ground.

Both creatures – the human and the demon – turned to face each other. The beast advanced at once, the ground shaking as he launched forward with each step on his trunk-like legs. The beast's eyes never left Stamwell and he did not see the blade held proud before him until his body impaled itself onto it.

*****

There was a moment of silence between them as the beast tried to understand what had happened. Stamwell had no idea if this creature had any perception of the world around him, any form of consciousness, but after what happened next, there would be no question that it knew what pain was.

Its eyes turned a paler shade of red as the blood drained from them and around its grotesque body. The ear-piercing shriek that followed deafened Stamwell, causing him to double up to protect the rest of his body from the vibrations that shattered his ear drums.

Stamwell, distracted by the ringing - and then bleeding – in his ears, did not see the arm swing towards him brandishing a fist full of black claws, tapered to a point as sharp and deadly as the head of a poisoned arrow. They sliced easily at Stamwell's flesh and opened his shoulder up as easily as a knife through warm butter. It happened so suddenly that there was no rush of blood immediately, for his heart had stopped for a second or two, draining his life supply back into itself, before spewing it back out around his body, easily finding the opening of the wound.

Stamwell staggered back a couple of paces, the heat from the strike coursing through his body, his entire right arm turning to pins and needles, going numb. His arm hung there, useless, as Stamwell found himself bowing before the beast unwittingly on a bended knee.

Apollyon pulled away, still shrieking but the sound now muffled to Stamwell due to the injury to his ears, as he struggled to control his breathing as well as slow the bleeding. His head was becoming weightless, his vision starting to blur, and he could see the looming figure of the beast returning to advance upon him. Its movements were shakier now and with every step taken, it squealed as it too was losing blood from the open wound in its stomach. As the beast had thrashed and sliced away at Stamwell, it had worked itself loose from the blade, but not before inadvertently twisting it several times to tear away at its own inners.

It may not have shared the human thought, but it was clear the beast knew pain, and even feared death itself. Stamwell, in his own stupor, briefly wondered whether the beast *could* die. Would that not have been the reason why the Council wanted to raise such abomination – to be able to provide, at last, an indestructible leader?

No.

Stamwell knew that one strike from a simple – but heavy – blade was not enough to render the beast at the mercy of its own god. Shadows loomed around Stamwell as it moved closer. It did not seem to take another step this time, but instead leapt towards where Stamwell crouched, where he was finally able to acquire enough oxygen to pull strength back into his limbs. His right arm now useless, Stamwell's left grabbed the sword from the floor and raised it as high as he could, his strength now sapping from the rest of his body as quickly as he was losing blood on his right.

His left arm jerked with the impact but remained rigid and taut for a moment more, as the weight of Apollyon bore down on him. The blade ran deep within its flesh once again, a slight crunch as it penetrated the armour-like exterior and then a squelch as it met the spongy flesh and muscle beneath.

The sound of crunching bone joined the cacophony, but Stamwell thought the weight was slowly crushing the bones in his own arm. He used the rest of his remaining strength to let go of the blade and drag his body quickly to the right, performing a clumsy commando roll. He heard the soft thud and clink as the metal of the blade finally hit the ground, pressed down by the unbearable weight of Apollyon's limp frame.

The beast had once again forced its own body on the blade, which had entered through the thinner flesh on the underside of its chin, riding through piercing its jaw, then the tongue and finally the roof of its mouth, meeting the nasal capacity before appearing again through the small area between its ghastly eyes.

It lay there limp but still snorting as it drew its final breaths. It did not appear to die, but Stamwell decided not to wait around to witness the finale. Both arms now felt useless to him, and betrayed his every move, but his legs were still his friends. They helped push his own massive frame from the floor and his heart was able to once again force blood to his injured limbs.

Stamwell could see the prisoner – now just another limp body amongst the debris that scattered the chamber floor – but he could hear the faint exhalations brush the dirt under where he lay, as the breath still struggled in and out. Stamwell staggered over to one of the mangled bodies of the Council members - not sparing a thought for the lost lives as they had all had it coming, he grabbed one of the thick, black hooded robes from beneath the corpse. Stamwell's near-superhuman strength returning to him, he wrapped the robe around his shoulders, hoisted Ewan's body, over his left shoulder and quickly headed for the exit.

He looked around the room once more, sparing a thought for the evil that the Council had raised – the still-snorting body of Apollyon laying on its front, its royal sceptre rising from the top of its head, covered in its own mix of grey and blood – as its hands began to claw once more and the earth around him. Stamwell spared a thought also for the man who he had loved, his Father in life – William Archibald – as his mutilated body lay surrounded, and covered in, the product of a life misled.

Stamwell turned and ran towards the darkness of the tunnel leading out of the cave. This time, he did not look back.

Chapter Twenty-Three

Stamwell welcomed the warmth rising throughout the day whilst he worked. The breeze was still cold at this time of year, particularly on the wide, unbroken expanse of Wildermoor but the sun chased away the chill and kept at bay the shivers he had woken with. As he did every day, he spent the hours breaking down the wilting and dead remnants of the winter harvest, to clear the ground for the next phase of growth. He wanted to make this land his own. Ewan had promised it to him and it would become the home he had promised Katrina.

He wondered if he was being led down a similar path once again. Was Ewan just building him up to cut – or chain – him down again? Was he to adhere to the needs that the Childs family history dictated rather than carve out a life of his own?

He banished the thoughts to the back of his mind. What nonsense. Ewan was indebted to him for saving his life and had rewarded him with a new start and the love of an angel. Why spoil it all with baseless paranoia? This was his new start.

He hacked away at more of the rotten greenery, as if he were hacking down the thoughts that taunted and the dreams that haunted him.

*****

As the sun slowly set beneath the heavy storm clouds gathering, Stamwell returned to the derelict steel structure of the barn that had once housed the prized herd of the famed Childs cattle. He wiped a mixture of dirt and dew from the blade of the scythe and placed it gently, proudly, in its rightful place on the back wall above the dusty workbench.   His thoughts ran for a moment back to a better time, years ago, when that place would have been the nerve centre for the family business; cattle reared and raised, prepared for the inevitable trip to the slaughterhouse. The crops growing strong from the tender ground. A cruel life, but an honest one. Ewan had explained that the entire village reaped the benefits during the winter months of a strong store of the finest beef and potatoes in the South West. The crops grown across the James plantation, combined with the Childs'' beef market, were supposed to have been the beginning of a new empire, as the two heads-of-house planned over many nights in the Weary Traveller.

Stamwell often sympathised with the cattle. It was a life that Stamwell was familiar with, having seen the streams of innocents marched through the corridors of the Ministry – the name Archibald bestowed upon the dark, damp and suffocating depths of the cavern below Devil's Pit. Many of the innocents were marched by Stamwell himself. He felt bitter about his past, blaming those around him for never offering him a life where sacrifice was actually rewarded. His parents, the Council, Archibald…the list went on.

Turning his attention back to the cooling air around him, Stamwell spied an envelope laying to the far right of the workbench. He picked it up and examined it. It was sealed with a red ribbon, his name written on the front in handwriting he recognised.

*****

With a trembling hand Stamwell managed to tear open the envelope and remove the page from within, his whole body rigid with apprehension and fear. Many a letter, written by the same hand, had passed through Stamwell to William Archibald. They had never born good news. Archibald had known that his brother Julius only contacted him with demands.

Julius mind had been far more poisoned than that of his brother's and Stamwell had always blamed him for his master's downfall. Aside from being a controlling, devious sibling, Julius also ruled the Council of Eternal Light with an iron and blood-stained fist.

Somehow, Julius and the remaining Council members had found where Stamwell was living. He doubted that Julius had been present that night in the cavern, as he never got his hands dirty, and had too high a standing to keep his face covered in the presence of the rest of the Council. He had no faith in his brother's ability to deliver on his promises, and Julius' absence that night had further displayed the distrust he held for William.

Stamwell stared at the words beautifully and carefully written on the page.

A son for a brother; a simple trade to cleanse the blood from your hands. Return home tonight, or we will claim her too. Come alone.

A son for a brother. William Archibald had made no secret he had viewed Stamwell as the heir he never sired. Stamwell understood the message loud and clear; Julius was asking for his life in exchange for that of his brother.

The second line of the letter took his breath away and caused him to tear the letter into pieces before bolting straight out of the barn, his legs not stopping until he reached the homestead of Tewke's Range. *Home* was not the house at the top of the hill; it referred to the pit and caves that he had left behind.

Katrina.

She had been peaceful in their bed when he rose that morning. She had not disturbed his day's toil with her usual cheery insistence that he come in for lunch. He had not thought this odd at the time. His efforts had been concentrated on clearing the remainder of the land ready for the next month''s harvest. He had thought she was spending the afternoon cooking the usual evening feast that would fill their bellies before they saw the rest of the night out at The Weary Traveller. That had quickly become the lovers' tradition.

The guilt was overwhelming as the dastardly thoughts and images plagued his mind all the way back to the house. He had left Katrina alone, unprotected, and had not given a second thought to the dangers that might await her.

It may already be too late. Stamwell readied himself for a second at the front door of the stone house. As he grabbed the brass handle to turn it, the pain in his shoulder returned, burning deep under the flesh and spreading. Stamwell's breath was shallow as he forced open the door and stood in the cold, odourless kitchen.

The only smell that filled his nostrils was light and coppery. A streak of blood traced from the staircase on the opposite side of the kitchen to where he stood at the door.

He screamed her name as he crossed the breadth of the kitchen with two steps. His voice echoed throughout the ground floor of the building but no reply came. He rushed between the rooms either side of the kitchen – the living room to the right and the cool, dark pantry to the left. There was no trace of Katrina.

He ascended the staircase two steps at a time yelling her name again. By the time he reached the landing at the top he knew she was gone. He could find no evidence she ever had been there. The bed was neatly made, the curtains open in each of the upper floor rooms as if she had greeted the new day and then vanished.

Stamwell lingered in their bedroom, his mind replaying the last moments they shared together that morning. It had all seemed so normal; so peaceful, so right. Why would he think anything could go wrong? He had changed so much within a week, letting his guard down; the very strength that William Archibald had beaten into him, in order to protect their underground coven. He had abandoned everything that had made him the protector in his previous life at Harper Falls.

Stamwell staggered towards Katrina's small dressing table that sat at the foot of the bed, his legs feeling weak. He stared into the gold-framed mirror. His face had become drawn, his eyes rimmed with black and his hair hung lank from his head. The image of him was of a man who no longer had the strength to hold himself together. As he stared at himself there was a faint titter inside his head. Laughter. *Cruel laughter.*

His shoulder still burned. He touched the flesh to convince himself he was not being consumed by flames. The pain pulsed when he touched the wound causing him to throw his arm back to his side.

Return home tonight.

There must be a chance. He could not let Katrina pay for his sins or for his negligence and betrayal to Archibald.

Stamwell tried walking away from the dresser but his legs buckled beneath him. As he fell to the wooden floor, his arm caught hold of the wardrobe door causing it to fly open as his weight pulled it behind him.

He hit the floor landing on his right hip but managed to catch himself in a half-sitting position. He stared up into the wardrobe and instantly the pain in his shoulder eased. His mind cleared of the fog that had clouded his thoughts. The hooded black gown hung like a beacon.

Stamwell hauled himself to his feet, grabbed the garment and threw it roughly over his head. The warmth returned to his body but did not burn like before. He suddenly felt he could breathe again. He stomped down the stairs, out of the front door and ran back to the barn.

He gazed around the length of the workbench, his feet pressing the pieces of the torn letter into the dirt as he marched over them. The written words were now buried in the earth, just as the words were buried deep in his soul and burned into his memory. They had awoken something deep within him, powering the cogs of something powerful, pumping a new resurgence of life through him.

Stamwell surveyed the collection of silver on the wall above him; blades each with their own design and purpose. But there was one that he felt compelled to call upon. *One he could trust.* It hung there like proudly where Stamwell had rested it less than an hour earlier. He still felt chills as he gazed lovingly at the tool that had become his showpiece since moving to Tewke's Range. Ewan had marvelled at how swiftly, concisely and expertly Stamwell handled the scythe.

Stamwell craned his body to lift it down from the wall and stood with it as he ran his hand up the full six-foot-tall shaft, caressing the top of the three-foot-long curved blade. The scythe was an extension of his power; the power that he had been promised all of his adult life.

Returning to the barn doors he stared out at Tewke's Range once more, knowing that it might be his last time. The sun remained high in the sky and despite the heat already radiating through the thick dark material shrouding his body, he pulled the heavy hood over his head. It hung low covering much of his face, so that all he could see was the earth passing beneath him. He set out across the land that with love he had rejuvenated over the last week. At least he would depart leaving behind new life in this place.

As he walked heavily across the field, covering half the distance within quarter of an hour, his thoughts returned to Katrina, the one who had stolen his heart and clouded his mind. He gripped the shaft of the scythe tighter. He would bring justice down on the Council, at any cost to himself, but not Katrina. No, she must return to Tewke's Range and carry on the work that they had promised they would carry together.

He should not have been expected to be able to run from his past or that it would never find him.

He had to move fast, there was much ground to cover that day; the same distance it had taken two battered bodies four days to cross when he and Ewan had fled the cave.

This time was different though. He knew where to go. He knew these woods better than most and as he pictured Julius Archibald's sneering face, his mind acted like a compass, leading him down the pathways and between the trees that would lead him to the Council.

By nightfall they would all die. But not his Katrina.

As he crossed the ground left between Tewke's Range and the forest edging towards Harper Falls, he heard someone calling in the far distance back from home.

They called a name but it was a name that he was steadily failing to recognise.

Chapter Twenty-Four

Ewan was in the cellar of The Weary Traveller when he saw her. He had excused himself from the ensuing lunchtime rush upstairs, claiming a barrel-change as his reason. Since he had woken that morning, he had been battling a headache that had now become a relentless pounding, the pain increasing behind his eyes, impairing his vision with intermittent flashes of bright spots. He hadn't suffered a migraine since he was a child and knew he needed the darkness and silence of the cellar to chase the pain away.

He propped himself up on an upturned barrel and willed his body to relax. He closed his eyes unsure whether what he saw was real. The darkness in the space blanketed all light that filtered down from the lively bar upstairs. The dark felt heavy today.

He forced his eyes open when a bright ethereal light started to creep from the cellar door at the top of the small wooden staircase. It seemed to float down the steps. Ewan was fixated on a figure, which grew closer.

That entire side of the cellar shone silver. Then she appeared.

Bathed in the warming light was a woman, sweet and slender, with an air of confidence and strength, her golden-brown hair hanging straight as diamonds to her waist. She walked slowly; her face at rest and peaceful.

"Katrina…" Ewan whispered, unable to comprehend that the figure resembled his sister. But there was no denying it; it was *her*.

"Katrina!" Ewan said the sound of his own voice startling him in the dark.

As quickly as she had appeared she had disappeared back into the darkness that filled the damp cellar.

The dark now felt heavier to Ewan and was starting to suffocate him.

The weight of the shadows lifted as Ewan ran up the staircase, back into the bright light and humdrum of the bar, which had reached its usual lunchtime capacity. He rushed past the tables laden with half-empty tankards, ignoring the greetings that a few of the regulars sent his way. He needed to get out of this place; he needed to get back to Tewke's Range. Something wasn"t right.

He launched onto the back of his stallion that was tethered to its hitching post in the courtyard of the pub and it lurched into a gallop, the horse sensing its master's apprehension. A short trek of two miles and they were home. Ewan stopped at the bordering fence at the rear of the property. He listened trying to hear the sound of voices that usually emanated from the house.

Nothing. An eerie silence.

Something glinted in the sunlight far into the range's main fields. Ewan squinted against the glare of the sun that was beating down onto his face. The figure, shrouded in black from head to toe, moved swiftly in the direction of the trees. The glint came from the metal of the huge blade it carried in its left hand.

He knew who the figure was. Only one man could stand that tall and walked slightly stooped, his right arm limply hanging by his side.

The hulk had confided that his mother had given him another name.

"Lucas!" Ewan hollered. The figure did not stir, did not turn towards him, did not deter from his path and did not slow down. Ewan yelled again but the figure was moving with blistering speed for his size and was soon lost under the cover of the forest.

Chapter Twenty-Five

Katrina"s body trembled uncontrollably as she was dragged to the centre of the pit. The hooded figures all around her stared blankly and in between her tears she could see they were exchanging nods of agreement. One figure stood at the centre of the small group of hidden faces, in a heavy white robe, his hood hanging down his back, his head and face bared proudly.

Although he towered over her where Katrina lay forced to the ground she could tell that he was not large in stature. But the way he held himself, shoulders back, head high, she knew he was in charge. His thick white hair cropped short. His eyes looked cold, his pupils the colour of icy pools. His face was thin, his cheekbones protruded and his mouth slight that broke into a grin of sadistic pleasure. Julius Archibald was a man who knew he was in control.

"Bring her to me," he commanded one of the hooded figures, too important to bend down and touch her himself.

Roughly Katrina was pulled to her feet. She groaned as she was forced to stand, struggling to bear weight on the leg that had been badly cut when she had tried to escape them at her home. The figures had appeared from nowhere whilst she tended to her morning household duties and everything since then had been a blur.

Along with the shock of the intrusion, the pain from her leg had caused her to pass out whilst being hauled across the fields towards the trees. Now, she was being manhandled again and forced to stand before Julius who looked her up and down. He repulsively ran his tongue across his smile, as he began to speak.

"Well, well," he said, addressing the remains of the Council, "It seems our boy has done alright for himself," he tittered menacingly towards the hooded figures that nodded again in agreement. "Shush, child," he patted her hair, holding his hand there much longer than necessary. Staring into his face she saw no flicker of life behind his eyes. No evidence of a soul.

"This can go one of two ways," he warned.

She struggled against his touch, resulting in the spectral figure holding her arms behind her back to twist a little more, showing how easily he could break her beautiful, sleek limbs if he was commanded to.

"Whilst we wait for your boyfriend" he spat the last word like it were an accusation or a sin, "When he decides to grace us with his presence, I need to know whether you're worth the sacrifice for him, or even worth saving." He sneered. "I am a busy man and will not be kept waiting."

He moved towards her then bowed his head closer to her neck. She struggled to stifle her sobs as she felt his tongue slither on her neck, his mouth closing over it, trapping her flesh beneath his teeth, as his hands began to explore her body. The more she squirmed against his touch, the harder her arms were held back. The pain became too much to bear so closed her eyes and tried desperately to block out the image of the evil that touched her.

Her eyes sprang open as Julius's head jerked back from her skin. A heavy, thump echoed within the circle. A woman's scream emerged from one of the dark hoods as they all stared at what had fallen from above into the centre of the pit. A crumpled, lifeless body, the black shroud glistening as the blood poured from an opening cut in its back. The head was missing. Katrina retched at the site of the mutilated body. All the hooded eyes and those of Julius Archibald trained towards the top of the pit walls, searching.

There stood the culprit, the murderer – a massive black shadow, also hiding beneath a hood, stood with a six-foot weapon by his side, the blade dripping with fresh blood.

Julius stared into the void of darkness that surrounded the upper wall of Devil's Pit and realised that he was staring into the night. The figure had evaporated into the shadows. The glimmer of light on the blade now dulled to darkness and the heat he had felt staring into those distant eyes – those red eyes – had cooled.

Chaos reigned around him, the frantic voices of the fellow Council members mingling with Katrina's hysterical cries as she tried in vain to pull away, to shield her eyes from the headless body that lay before her. Julius remained calm. It was his duty to reinstall order to the evening's proceedings.

He looked up and called into the night,

"The more blood you spill the easier my decision will be, boy. This –", he growled as he grabbed Katrina by the neck and puller her in front of him, "She means nothing to me if you continue to fight us!"

A heavy rustle emerged from within the trees at the base of the pit where they stood and startled everyone. The Council members could no longer conceal their fear behind the heavy fabric masks they hid behind. Their bodies were shrunken, shoulders hunched and hands clasped together in an attempt to comfort themselves. Their heads darted from left to right with every tiny sound that called from the forest around them.

Julius held Katrina to him and stood behind her, his arm wrapped around her neck in a loose stranglehold ensuring she did not escape his clutches.

The trees began to move as a powerful breeze slowly and deliberately blew through them. Then the figure emerged from the shadows once more. Julius' eyes fell wide and his grip on Katrina slackened for a few moments, as he struggled to absorb the size of the figure moving towards him. He had not seen Stamwell since he was a teenager. His brother had always raved about the boy's strength and size. The boy was now a man – more than a man for he moved like a god. He moved without fear. The black shroud he was draped in made his frame look even larger and more frightening and only his eyes could be seen from deep within the void. They were no longer the same eyes that had shone like gems when they looked at Katrina at Tewke's Range. They shone fire-and-blood red.

Julius heard Katrina gasp as she was forced to look inside the hood.

"Not too close," Julius warned. "That's far enough."

Still Stamwell proceeded forwards.

"A son for a brother, remember?" Julius quoted the note he had left Stamwell. Stamwell's body was reacting to the rage that was coursing through it. Underneath the hooded cloak his body ran with sweat and his fever soared.

Julius reached under his own robe, behind where Katrina's body pressed against him and withdrew a knife, its blade crude and dangerously serrated. He reached into the waistband of Katrina's skirt, pulled the tails of the blouse out and bared her stomach. He took time to run his cold fingers across her smooth, white flesh before resting the ugly blade of the knife against it.

"*Your* son, Lucas," said Julius coldly, "for my brother, if you will not give your life for his."

Stamwell took another stride towards Julius, his body trembling underneath the robe he wore. He ached, not just with the fever and infection setting in, but with blind rage and panic for the life of the woman he loved. Julius pressed the blade into Katrina's flesh, instantly drawing a slither of blood.

The cry of pain halted Stamwell in his tracks. He stood unmoving, staring Julius down and wanting to tear him apart.

"This," said Julius signalling with his hand the arrangement of heavy wooden posts, adorned with lit flame torches, the trunk which stood in the centre of the clearing "is all for you, Stamwell. It's for the good of humanity. You carry within you the seeds of evil, which you have passed on to your whore," he growled taking the opportunity to run his tongue once more against Katrina's neck. "The child – this evil – belongs to us and we shall reclaim it."

Stamwell move forward another step. He was ready to lunge at Julius and gut him with his own knife, spilling whatever insides he possessed before systematically taking him apart with the blade with which he had already silenced one Council member.

But he couldn't. He knew he mustn't. He had reached the end of the line. Seeing Katrina cower against Julius, squirming at his touch with a look of horror on her face was killing him inside.

He had to end it now, to save her.

Stamwell relented, held out his arms wide to his side and let the scythe fall to the ground. He submitted himself to evil itself. He lowered his hood slowly finally looking Katrina in the eye. He wanted to tell her so much, to ask if she was indeed carrying his – *their* - child. But he knew it was true and somehow Julius knew it too.

Stamwell's eyes silently pleaded with Katrina for forgiveness. Katrina's eyes were fixed on the side of Stamwell's face that had succumbed to what was taking over his body. The skin had hardened forming scale-like armour around his eye-socket and had spread down across his cheek meeting the corner of his mouth. His eyes were bloodshot and dark-rimmed.

"It's already begun," Julius said in wonder staring at his face.

All of Stamwell's resolve was slowly dying and when Julius nodded to one of the two hooded figures behind the man-mountain, he neither moved nor fought against it as the man repeatedly sank a knife into his flesh. Stamwell's shoulders and back opened up as he sank to his knees, his eyes never leaving Katrina's face, never ceasing to ask for forgiveness.

"Ready the pyre," Julius bellowed.

*****

"I arrived too late," The tears were welling and stinging Truman's eyes.

"You remember," Evelyn replied, more a statement than a question.

Truman – *Ewan* – nodded his head slowly, his eyes closing and the first of the tears falling from his face. He sat on the floor in the white room holding his legs close to his chest.

"What happened?" Evelyn asked, "Tell me."

Truman knew that Evelyn was aware of how that night had ended and did not need to be told but Truman felt he owed her and himself to recall the memories, which for centuries had remained hidden.

"It took my sister weeks before she could tell me. She was in shock, lived in silence, locked in mourning. She gave up on life but carried on breathing. I found her out by the lake one morning just staring at the water looking for answers. She told me that she was looking for a way out; a way back to Lucas."

Evelyn sat next to him, her hand on his spurring him on.

"The white-haired man – the leader – believed that Lucas had been infected by the beast from the cave; that its evil was manifesting in him. He seemed obsessed by the idea that this saviour must be set free from Lucas' body. They had pretty much taken his life before they tied him to the post. It had all been arranged – the logs situated at the bottom of the post, the lanterns lighting the Pit. They were doing what they had always done, rituals held in darkness, in secret in that Pit, hoping to raise their demonic saviour, at the cost of innocent lives. They had it all planned out."

The tears fell but Truman's voice strengthened as he carried on, the painful memories finally flowing free as the dam broke down.

"They tore off his robe and cut deep into his scars. Whatever it was that was taking over Lucas's body was killing his flesh from within. They opened up more wounds to allow the demon to escape."

"When was that?"

Truman's head fell again into his hands. He sobbed into them as the past came to life.

"When they lit the fire beneath him; making my sister watch him burn. I heard Katrina's cries before I reached the Pit. It killed me to hear it too. Every moment they tortured him, it tortured her."

A silence lay between them as Truman tried once more to fight his way through the images of his past.

"I failed them both, Evelyn." He ignored the insistent shaking of her head. "I was not there to save either of them. The man saved my life once and saved my sister's by giving her hope and I just let him die."

Evelyn tried reaching out for Truman's hand but he shrugged her off violently, startling her. He turned away from her, brought his knees to his chest and lay in a foetal position weeping on the warm, pulsing floor. His chest heaved as he struggled to catch his breath in between his sobs. There was no end for his sorrow. The torture had begun again.

He wept until his eyes were dry and they finally closed. The light disappeared leaving Truman again in darkness.

Chapter Twenty-Six

Truman finally woke in the darkness. His shirt was dried to his skin, held there by a combination of endless tears, saliva, mucus and sweat. He felt as though he had woken from a deep sleep brought on by a fever. His head hurt as he tried to focus his eyes, looking to bring forth the light once more.

He missed the warmth and safety of the white room. He had not woken up there since that day with Evelyn and every day since had found himself in the cool, damp walls of his stone cell. He had lost track of how many days, weeks or months had gone by in that place.

But something was different this time. He no longer felt totally alone. *Worse*, he thought; he felt as though he was being watched.

As he sat up on the thin mattress, his joints creaking as they adjusted with the cold, he could see two white spheres light up in the opposite corner of his tiny room. The shapes – eyes – moved closer to greet him, sparkling in the light. The spectacles covering them slipped forward slightly as they did so and were caught by the crooked end to the nose they rested on.

"Welcome back, Mr Childs," the voice soothed, "we have been waiting a long time for you to return to us."

Truman stared into the darkness as the voice spoke trying to place it. He knew he recognised it. With the sound of the voice, his body grew colder. The voice was comforting, chilling and menacing all at once. There was only one other time Truman remembered having that feeling.

"Stamford?" Truman replied.

"I'm glad you're back. I hope you're well rested as you're going to be helping us." The white of the doctor's teeth shone in the darkness as his smile beamed.

It was not a request. It barely resembled a command. It was a threat; the emptiness behind Stamford's eyes gave away his true intentions almost immediately. In his own mind, Truman had already risen to his feet, had descended on the still frame of the doctor and had circled both his hands around the man's throat, squeezing out the last of the pathetic life that the doctor had left, in exchange for the little life Truman had left.

In reality, Truman only raised his arms an inch before the iron chain pulled taut once more and gripped him in a vice, waiting the next strike of the hammer or serration of a rusty blade. He was at the mercy of the demented doctor.

Stamford let out a small sigh, almost a laugh, as Truman struggled in his shackles. A dim light was beginning to illuminate the rest of the cell and his eyes slowly grew accustomed to his new surroundings. Stamford – or whomever he had called to bring Truman's comatose body to this place – had been kind enough to prop Truman up at the head of the metal-framed cot in a sitting position, held in place by the cold bare stone wall behind. This enabled Truman to remain properly oriented when he came around. He realised that panic would have only worsened the situation.

"Don't struggle, Mr Childs."

"Why do you call me that?"

"Why wouldn't I? It is who you were, who you still are in essence today," Stamford replied calmly. "You have seen it for yourself."

"I have seen nothing but ravings and hallucinations brought on by whatever drug you have administered to me."

An outburst sprang from the back of Stamford's throat, a scoff at Truman's naivety.

"Think what you will about those events, Mr. Childs, but they were real. There is no getting away from that fact. As sure as night becomes day, you were – *are* – Ewan Childs and you *will* help us," Stamford re-iterated. "You are the only one left who can."

That last statement alerted something within Truman. He brushed aside the notion for a second before deciding, maybe yes, quite possibly…Dr. Mason Stamford sounded scared. Up until this point, the doctor had held his voice strong with an air of confidence and menace that hung in the ether between the two men, neither of which who now believed the threat existed at all. Stamford's voice had trembled and betrayed him.

Now it was Truman's turn to scoff and mock.

"*You* brought me here, wherever this place is. You've put images in my head that I don't know if I believe are real or if I was just hallucinogenic. You have caused me to slowly question my own sanity, and then you insult the tattered remains of my integrity by asking for *my* help!" Truman stopped long enough to catch his breath once more. "My God, man, you really are pathetic," he spat the words in Stamford's direction, replicating the words from their previous encounter in the staged psychiatrist's surgery.

The venom returned to Stamford as he responded, fuelled now by the hatred and pity he held for the man who sat before him, dishevelled and helplessly shackled to a rusty cabin bed in a dank holding cell.

"I never asked," he said slowly, letting each word slither off his tongue. "Rather, I *told* you that you were going to help us. I never said you had a choice."

Truman's arms again instinctively wanted to launch towards the doctor's exposed neck, but only shook the chains, strengthening their impenetrable hold on his wrists. He gave in to their iron grip and let his head fall back against the cold wall once again. He closed his eyes and tried searching for the answers that he knew were hidden within the shadows somewhere. He wanted to return to the white room, or to Tewke's Range, where everything had made sense to him.

"What do you want from me?" He asked, his eyes still closed attempting to shield himself from the harsh reality he had woken up to.

There was no response. His head fell to his chest and he prised his eyes open once more. As the light continued to rise within the cell, the flame from a torch flickered against Stamford's frame, huddled tightly in the chair at the foot of the bed. For the first time Truman was able to observe the man's face.

Whatever fear had gripped and manifested Stamford's speech a few moments ago was physically wearing the man down. Darkness circled his eyes and the skin on his face had started to sag. The man looked as though he had not slept for weeks.

Stamford's lifeless eyes stared back at him, the light continuing to showcase the lines that ran down his face, deep creases in the pale skin. Stamford's hair was now white, riddled with flecks of black. There had only been the distinguished badger-stripes of silver at his temples when they met previously.

Whatever was happening in Stamford's mind had aged him far beyond his years. It had happened within the days or weeks since the day at the surgery.

"A means to an end," Stamford said finally. "You are the key to a new beginning for all of us," he continued before Truman could muster the words to question him. "You can either choose to help me and join us or…" his voice trailed off, as he lifted both hands and motioned around the torturous cell surrounding them.

A shiver ran through Truman making him tremble uncontrollably. The faint flicker of the candle had started to warm Truman's face but there was not enough life in the flame to transfer the heat he needed to his lower body. He sat chained to his cot and watched Stamford rise to his feet and walk towards the wall onto which his bed was bolted. He stood a few feet from the bed as Truman heard a latch come free and the creak of old, tired hinges, groaning with effort, as the battered wooden shutters were pulled open.

Due to his immobility, Truman had not registered that the room had a window. As the shutters were drawn back clattering against the stone wall beside his head, Truman welcomed the ray of light and rush of warmth that raced in through the window to the centre of the room before settling on a spot in the middle of the concrete floor. It rested at Stamford's feet like a forlorn but loyal family puppy cowering before its master.

"In twelve hours, I will present you to my superiors," he gazed wistfully out of the window into whatever world rested outside, "You will be my greatest triumph; the missing link."

Truman's pulse quickened and his breathing grew shallower as he listened to the doctor's premature victory speech. Something was happening. At that very moment, someone's demented plans were whirring into action. What horrified Truman the most was that he had no idea what, or with whom, he was dealing. Chained to the unforgiving and uncomfortable bed in apparent solitary confinement, he had little chance to find out unless he acted quickly.

The fear, the cloudiness of his mind and the frustration were beginning to boil inside him. As he closed his eyes, the images of the flames consuming Stamwell's body returned, the heat searing his cheeks as he stared into their fiery embrace; he did not want to return to that time, the life he once had. The shadows of the past brought fear and he needed the light of hope.

But he needed to face these demons if he had any chance of finding out what was going to happen. First thing"s first, he needed to find a way off this bed, out of this room and back into the world he once knew.

With regret he knew he needed to meet Stamford on his level whether he believed in anything that was going on in this man's mind or not.

"What happened to him after the fire?"

Stamford's head met Truman's, finally torn from the sanctuary he had found on the other side of the window. He smiled, wryly.

"So you *do* believe?"

"You told me that it was all real, so why question me now?" Truman fired. "I need to know what happened."

As pride gleamed over his face, the colour seemingly returning to his old skin, Stamford met Truman's inquisition with wonder.

"Oh, great things," he purred. "He is on a higher plane than us, now."

"I know he died," reasoned Truman wanting to know more than the obvious facts. "No one could have survived that kind of fate."

"He did not die," Stamford spoke in a hushed whisper, "We made him a god."

"Stamwell was everything that William Archibald wanted in a son," Stamford's gaze returned to the outside world. "Everyone in the Council always said that was the Father's weakness – the need for an heir, for someone who could return the love that he had lost when his wife had been taken, forcing him to find solace in the quiet of the forest. They said that he cared too much how he was perceived in the boy's eyes to really make a serious play for leadership. His brother Julius on the other hand was different. He cared for no-one but himself and the Council, although his concerns never stretched to the individual members who had voted him into power. He wanted to use them to ascend, to become a higher power."

Sensing that this was not going to be a short account, Truman relaxed his arms to relieve the tension in his shoulders. Stamford, for the moment at least, posed no threat to him whilst he lost himself in his tale. Truman noticed that the doctor's eyes were unblinking; staring out into the serenity outside his cell. The reflection of the sun onto Stamford's face gave the impression that he was finally relaxing, the years starting to fall away from him as he spoke.

"The fire that took away William's wife, home and the chance of the family he yearned for, was of course started by Julius. We all knew it."

Truman's attention turned towards Stamford. So this was the man"s truth? He had been there too. They had both been part of the horrific scenes from that night in the forest. Truman now questioned his own sanity more than ever. He had placed Stamford in the mentally vacant category but now they seemed to share the same vision of a time lost long ago.

"When the order came from Parliament – who barely knew of our existence down here in Wildermoor – to adopt a new style of worship and religion, Julius rebelled instantly. It was almost as if this was the calling he had been waiting for; the purpose that he had been silently serving and working towards for years. He saw it as a sign from his own God to carry out his work for a new world order."

Stamford's words started to soften and fade in Truman's ears, becoming nothing more than a rhythmic humming in the background. As Truman remained propped against the cell wall, his arms hanging limp beside him, his hands had been meaninglessly folding the slack on the chain treating them as a set of makeshift rosary beads, praying to a god that he doubted existed. The darkness was beginning to form around him, his eyes remained open but his mind grew heavy as fatigue set in.

As his thumb and forefinger lovingly rolled over the chain a spark lit behind his eyes and again the room was bathed in light. Stamford's words returned to him with clarity but he remained distracted by the chain in his fingers. Something felt strange about it as he rolled the same section of chain through his fingers making sure his face and body appeared tired and disinterested. His mind tried to make sense of the messages that were travelling up the length of his arm attempting to form a picture in his mind.

The chain was still cold but warming to his touch. The metal was abrasive with rust but something had awoken his senses. Nothing felt odd about the chain at all until his thumb and finger gripped the same two links of the chain again. This time he recognised what his hands were feeling; a gap, so small he had to concentrate to feel it but a gap nonetheless.

A weak link.

The relief, excitement and apprehension flowed through his body, bringing new warmth to every fibre in him. Little by little, his body returned from its slumber. His arms wanted to flail and his legs kick out in a concerted effort to break the chain.

It's only one link though. He kept telling himself that. One sudden movement alone would not break his shackles and would probably tear the skin around his wrist whilst ripping his other arm from its socket.

No, he had to think this through. *Keep the man talking.* The doctor would reach the end of his story soon enough and Truman scarcely had time to act.

Gripping the break in the link between his two strongest digits, the thumb and forefinger, Truman managed to shield the broken section of chain with the rest of his hand. The rust on the chain rubbed against his skin as his fingers worked frantically and covertly. It would surely give soon.

"The boy's mother was one of William's first…subjects," Stamford remained unaware. "It was one of the only expeditions where William joined in with the Fielders. Once his men had dragged her away from the house, he heard the innocent cries of the boy upstairs - scared and now all alone and William could not bear to leave him. The boy had been too grief-stricken and frozen with shock to notice that he was being taken away. Over the next few weeks he had been treated like a prince. When they had moved deeper underground William had given the boy his own quarters.

The boy's strength grew second-to-none. We all observed it. William knew he had an asset that he could use, a son he could raise to help him gain the power he had been promised by his brother. The boy grew to protect the old man, never questioning his motives or actions. He had been given strength, family and a purpose. He offered loyalty in return. That was all William wanted and it was the only thing Stamwell needed to become the man he truly was. The one that he would become again."

Truman stifled any pain that was setting into his fingers as the rust started slicing deeper into the skin, his fingers now struggling to keep a grip on the chain as the blood started to pool from the small wound. Stamford's eyes still stared out of the window, giving Truman the opportunity to let out a silent sob enough to relieve the tension and keep him powering through.

Stamford suddenly brought his face back towards Truman, bringing his fingers to a halt. He gripped the chain firmly in his hand as he tried to regain the composure he had so valiantly displayed up until then.

"The day William was given the Ascension Rite, was the day they both sealed their fate," he said coldly staring deep into Truman's tired eyes.

As Truman tried to stop the trembling that had started in his arms from the effort he heard a faint clink as the link snapped between his fingers.

Chapter Twenty-Seven

The silence was deafening. It hung in the air between them and Truman could feel the weight of it undulate as Stamford's cold gaze fixed on him. He could feel – *hear* – the tension swing back and forth as if hanging from an invisible pendulum, its weight waiting to drop as it gathered speed.

A struggle whirled as Truman wrestled to maintain his composure, his own breathing quickening and threatening to betray him.

You've blown it, the voice berated him. *He's on to you.*

He heard nothing, another said reassuringly. *He was too caught up in the sound of his own voice. Just stay calm.*

In the end the poise that had made Truman such an effective, feared detective and interrogator started to win through. He urged Stamford to continue, undeterred. When no words came from Stamford, Truman realised he needed to make the first move.

"What happened that night in the caves? What was that…thing?" he asked calmly, despite his body shivering. Any warmth that was contained between the two men in the cold cell had now dissipated and Truman's breath was turning to light fog. He thought he saw the flicker of a smile appear across the doctor''s lips.

"Apollyon…" The reply was painfully hushed.

"What *was* it?" Truman pressed. The pretence becoming easier for him, as his mind flooded with the images he had been exposed to in the white room, memories that had been repressed since he had woken just as they had for centuries; memories that he was desperately trying to deny were real.

"A mistake. It was meant to be our new beginning," Stamford's voice trailed off as he stared into nothingness, appearing to be hypnotised by the corner of the wall behind Truman's bed. Suddenly, his eyes came alive once more; a switch flicked on inside him as he broke from his trance. Steadiness returned to his voice.

"Julius Archibald had grown attached to the idea of an underworld since his early teens or rather it grew attached to him. His movement into the church was merely a platform for him to acquire and groom a band of disciples who would follow him in his quest for a better world." Stamford's gaze fell to the floor and he let out a short snigger. "Ironic really, but it was what he wanted to achieve that set him aside from everyone else in his field. He would stop at nothing."

Stamford appeared to become more human as he spoke, his voice softening as he recalled the warm, sunny days from his past.

"An ancient book of rites came into his possession years later, and he became obsessed with one in particular; one that would raise the King of Locusts, The Destroyer. To Julius, he was not a ruler of the underworld but God's own bodyguard. He thought he was on course to carry out our Lord's work."

"Legend foretold of an angel who, if brought back to Earth, would reign for five months over a world of chaos, punishing those who did not follow or believe in God's will. To Julius, the Reformation Act of 1668 was evil in its purest form – a vain attempt by Parliament to erase hundreds of years of Christianity, to create a new religion simply to justify their own crimes. He became obsessed with taking them down and fighting for the God he had devoted his life to. Raising Apollyon would answer his and *our* prayers to return to a greater life. He promised William – the weaker brother - eternal life and power if he could succeed in raising the New Saviour. After years of planning, research and failed attempts, the night finally came and the stage was set."

"Set for what?" Truman no longer needed to mask his interest in what the doctor was saying. Stamford looked up slowly raising his head.

"Ascension," he responded, a haunting air of deliberation surrounding the single word, "and the birth of our new existence."

"What was the purpose of all this? What were *you* supposed to achieve?" Truman spoke harshly. He watched as Stamford's eyes dropped, the maniacal flame behind them faded and cooled. Despair washed over the doctor's face, his eyes darting from side to side trying to seek the right answer. Despair turned to disbelief as he pondered the answer.

"Salvation, of course," his voice starting to tremble, stifling a tear that stung behind his dead stare.

"At the cost of so many others?" Truman shot back, his confidence starting to return. "That is sacrifice, murder even. Not salvation."

"All sins are repented through sacrifice. It is the only way."

"You're talking about a higher power that rewards heartless acts of violence, torture and murder – motived by greed and power – rewarded with the empty promise of eternal life." Truman's mind was spinning, he was unsure whether he awake or even in the dark room. Was he even still alive?

The flame had reignited behind Stamford's stare, his face appeared carved from stone, his skin ashen. Truman knew that it would not be long before this man would become a raging inferno with his words acting as fuel.

"Don't pretend you have not dreamed of a life like this, Childs – eternal life, immortality," he sneered, addressing Truman with the name he possessed in a previous life. "A select few have experienced it and no-one can comprehend peace such as this."

"Knowing you're a murderer?"

"Mark my words. I, myself, have never taken another life, Mr Childs."

"Except that of Lucas Stamwell." The words slid off his tongue as if gliding over wet silk. Truman had cut through Stamford's armour piercing the skin. Now he wanted to go deeper beneath the flesh. "You took that man's life – a man I regarded as a brother. He stood alone against your kind, against the life of misguidance that had been bestowed upon him. A man brought up under the law of the unlawful, of the megalomaniacal. He wanted nothing more than his own life – an honest life, a life of truth." Truman stopped momentarily bringing his breathing under control. "A life my sister could have given him."

"No man should have to live a life so lonely to devote it to any other person than himself," Stamford whispered. "Every man deserves power, a chance to create his own destiny and rule his own world, no matter how vast or small it may be. But this can only be achieved by making the right choices."

"So you took it upon yourselves to choose it for him? To force upon him once more an existence he did not want."

"His destiny was written the night of the Ascension. He was chosen. We merely set him free."

The silence hung once more between them adding extra weight to the tension that continued to thicken. Truman ran his fingers through the broken chain. He comforted himself with the thought that he still had one more ace to play when the time came. The waiting was now making his nerves ache.

He wanted to close his eyes and return to a place not consumed by dark or blinded by light. Somewhere safe. Somewhere quiet. In order to return to a place like that he would have to break the silence.

"What becomes of *your* soul after all of this? Who will save you?"

Once again the ferocity in Stamford's stare began to die. Truman thought he could see a glint of light appear in the corner his eyes. It was a tear forming. It streaked and fell from Stamford's cheek, as he stood motionless, staring at nothing.

No more tears followed; no sobs. Truman had to strain to convince himself that the man was still breathing. He fought the urge to ask him if he was okay. His concern for Stamford's wellbeing was beginning to rise. Physically, he seemed in perfect shape for a man his age but, mentally this man was not well.

Eventually, Stamford's eyes began to move and the muscles in his face started to contract and loosen again. Within the short time since Truman had regained consciousness he had witnessed Stamford's demeanour change at least four or five times. He thought back to their first meeting and how quickly he had turned from the warm, welcoming health worker to a crazed psychopath worried Truman.

His eyes stared at the floor, then quickly darted and fixed on the wall behind Truman. Truman had the urge to turn around and find the source of Stamford's fixation but in doing so would have freed his right arm from its supposed position shackled to the bed frame giving the game away completely.

Looking into Stamford's face as much as he could in the rapidly fading light he saw that beneath the surface of his skin floated hundreds of souls, all trying to break free and make themselves known. His reactions to comments Truman had made – the bipolar nature of them – was as if each soul was called forward to answer for him.

Had Stamford brought this unfortunate affliction on himself or was he too being controlled?

Truman was brought back from the comforting depths of his own mind when the silence was finally broken.

"Our fates have already been written…" Stamford's voice rasped, his speech the only movement across his whole body, his eyes still staring over Truman's left shoulder. There was something else about the way he said it. The man actually sounded frightened. "We all serve a purpose to work towards a greater good and serve a higher power." It sounded like he was reciting a mission statement. Stamford swallowed loudly trying to lubricate his dry throat. They both felt the heat rise within the cell despite the cold walls still glistening with damp. The moisture in each man felt as though it were slowly evaporating.

Truman closed his eyes against the growing warmth trying to transport himself back to his happy place. But nothing worked. The heat fuelled the visions he had when he opened his eyes. He found himself standing alone in the middle of a vast plain somewhere across the scarred face of Wildermoor. The shadows slowly raising from the ground, growing to heights of six-foot and more, the lowest trails of the darkness transforming into two separate slithers of black, becoming more solid as they morphed into legs. As Truman looked around pin-pricks of red appeared, disappeared and then re-appeared. Thousands of red burning eyes stared at him hungrily.

The dark figures parted revealing one much larger. This one was made of more material – a trailing black robe, topped with a heavy hood, masking the face below. The weapon in his hand was familiar; a large curved blade atop a tall oak shaft.

These figures were not the most disturbing element of his vision. As he looked around him, the faint shrieks grew louder behind him – the screams of hundreds of souls.

Burning.

He could smell it. The fields were ablaze around him. He could feel the heat cooking his skin, his cheeks growing tighter, followed by the skin under his eyes and around to the back of his neck. He was starting to burn along with all of the poor souls who had been left behind.

And he was powerless to stop any of it, to stop the hooded figure from advancing. The Reaper had found him and was coming for him.

The vision was taken over by the brightest white light – another he recognised but did not fear. Evelyn would come with the light to take him away and make him safe again.

Truman's eyes flew open as he gasped, trying to refill his lungs. He was once again surrounded by darkness, the air feeling as chilled as it was before. And Stamford still stood before him staring, barely present at all.

The vision woke Truman's senses more than ever been before. Suddenly everything became clear to him. And that was what frightened him most of all. It was the knowing.

His body started to tremble again uncontrollably. He turned towards Stamford, determined to break him from his trance, believing at last he knew the truth.

"They're going to kill you, aren't they? If they don''t get what they want. That's what you're scared of."

Stamford's eyes moved and fixed on Truman's.

"Everybody is going to die. They have what they want. It has already begun."

Truman looked down at himself, still chained to the bed, forgetting he had a chance of escape. One free arm was no good. He felt powerless to save himself, as he had centuries ago, unable to stop the inevitable.

"What purpose do *I* serve in all of this?" He pleaded.

Stamford's head cocked back up straight atop his neck, the lights seeming to come back on in his mind, again as though Truman had found an invisible switch. He responded with a sick smile, rolling off his forked tongue.

"You don't have one."

The words did not mean anything to Truman. He barely noticed that the doctor had spoken. His attention was locked squarely on the item in Stamford's right hand and the syringe, larger than the last one, with a needle four inches in length, as he advanced towards where Truman lay.

Helpless.

Once more Truman failed to believe he could stop what was about to happen to him. The doctor was upon him with two steps, too quickly for Truman to act. He could think of no smart way to escape this time for there wasn't one. He was chained up like an animal about to be euthanized. Every movement played out in slow motion but still it felt too quick for him to act.

He had forgotten about his free arm. His hand, still bloodied from the effort it took to break the weakened chain, waited until Stamford bowed his head and then flew from its broken restraints. His closed fist landed against Stamford's temple sending him sprawling backwards, his right hip taking the brunt of the fall. The blow lacked a significant amount of strength, but the shock was enough to daze the doctor for a few moments before he managed to gather his senses, amongst a string of breathless obscenities thrown at Truman.

Truman had to make the most of the brief respite and decided to use his free arm to attempt to loosen the shackles on his left, not yet knowing how he was possibly going to break through another chain. In that time Stamford got to his feet and had re-assumed his position.

Truman tried to raise his arm finding that it did not respond. He tried again frantically to wake the limb. It was no use. It simply would not move. He looked down to see the needle buried in his forearm and a wave of nausea overcoming him so suddenly that his head fell back against the wall. The pain dulled as he stared at the appendage protruding from his arm. The plunger was fully compressed and every ounce of whatever was in the syringe now coursed through his body.

He expected the darkness to ascend on him as quickly as it had done in the surgery, the last time that Stamford had injected him with whatever evil he had mastered into liquid form. Truman found himself welcoming the warmth, the glow, of the white room once more. He wanted to return there now more than ever.

But neither the darkness nor the light came to him. That's when he knew that something was very wrong.

Chapter Twenty-Eight

The warmth was comforting, coaxing him into a false sense of security. It started by flowing upwards from the entry point of the needle, quickly spreading up to his shoulders. He could feel it buzzing through his veins for only a second before he slowly started to relax.

"The beauty of the common lethal injection," Stamford said, his voice joining the deep thrum that was now pulsating in Truman's ears, "is that it is administered in three stages, supposedly to make it more humane but since when do criminals deserve the right to die humanely? If they have betrayed the ways of the Lord, they deserve to be thrown into the pits of hell!"

Stamford's eyes were rimmed red, looking tired and angry. The wild stare had not left his face, as if the pain in his head from the fall did not faze him. He gave Truman another cursory look, rolling his eyes briefly displaying his annoyance.

But this is exactly what you wanted, a voice told him in a hushed, gravelly whisper. *This was the way you always dreamed it to be.*

He concentrated on the patient on the bed before continuing.

"Sodium thiopental is used to induce unconsciousness, so that the *patient* is unaware of their body shutting down. This you have already experienced," an avaricious smile plastered his lips, "the day we met at my surgery. You - or should I say I – have no need for you to have this again. I proved to them that a controlled amount of this substance, together with the same of the second element, pancuronium bromide, can take patients to an unconsciousness so deep it takes them to the brink of death, the white light people speak of. You know better than others what is actually contained within that light."

He looked at Truman waiting for a response, but Truman could only stare blankly at him, drool starting to seep from the corner of his open mouth, as his body remained paralyzed. Truman could hear the doctor speak but could no longer make sense of the words.

His breathing started to suffer as his body tried to fight the invasion, unable to match its ferocity. Like Truman's mind, his body was succumbing to the warmth and the strange feeling of final peace washing over him. His eyes moved frantically as his limbs froze. He could see Stamford standing in front of him touching the open gash on his cheek. The chain must have caught his skin as his fist hit his temple, dragging the rusted barbs of the broken links across his face.

"The Others, Mr Darke," Stamford addressed him as the DI he had been at his surgery. "The ones who will try to take you from us, who will try to convince you that you are someone other than what you are, that you can be more than…" he struggled to find the words, as he looked at Truman, "More than *this*," he signalled at Truman's limp body.

The most disturbing aspect of this sensation was the very absence of pain. His body was not screaming out as he imagined it would during the onset of death. He had always envisioned he would be on the receiving end of a nasty head wound or gunshot to the stomach, something more dramatic – more heroic – than this

"What you should be feeling by now," Stamford continued with the lucidity of a college professor addressing a lecture, "is the power of my latest concoction – an elevated dose of pancronium bromide together with a kick of potassium chloride – the final two elements of a lethal injection. In the States they believe that these should be given separately to put the *felon* to sleep. What I have discovered is that just the right amounts of both bring on a euphoric high, an unparalleled feeling of being at peace, which last for a few moments before your body cannot compete any longer. The difference between how I conduct this practice, compared to those who supposedly do so to protect us from evil, is that you get to witness your own demise. You will still feel regret, remorse, fear and everything right up until the final moment. Your mind is the last thing to be taken over by the drug. It remains fully awake for the entire procedure. Just when there is only a thread of your life left, when you are willing death to come and take you away, *they* will come for you. That, Mr Darke, is what I have been hired to do. To create the link between your kind and theirs – to bring forth the next stage of our salvation."

No harm in enlightening him now. Within a few minutes it would not matter. No one can stop us now.

His smile lingered as he basked in the glory of it, the culmination of years of work, dedicated to this one patient, this one moment. He closed his eyes for a few seconds to revel in it all.

Truman cursed himself whilst he still could for wasting a few precious moments feeling sorry for Stamford. His initial gut feeling about him had been right – this man was severely unhinged. Truman's own instincts had betrayed him. Years of police training that had taught him to be mindful, if not suspicious of everyone around him, had faded since that night he had been chased from Colin Dexler's house and branded a crooked cop and a murderer by his own men.

That moment, Truman decided, had started the clock that now ticked down his final moments. From then he had lost all judgment and awareness to any danger that days before he would have smelt coming from miles away. That felt like a lifetime ago. Just another one to add to his apparent history of failed existences.

Once a pillar of this community, one of the most admired, respected and feared men in Wildermoor now lay wasting away on a dirty bed in a damp cell, outsmarted by one of Hell's henchmen.

The poison Stamford had sent forth to claim his soul was now sinking its teeth in and taking hold. Truman lay in the jaws of fate waiting for one God or another – either his or Stamford''s – to claim the scraps that were left of him.

The warmth rose in one final surge from his toes, running up his legs and to his stomach, pushing twisted euphoria through his veins, absorbing into his vital organs and running through his bloodstream. Once the feeling reached his face the shivers started as his vital organs began to malfunction. His blood pressure and heart rate rose to deadly levels, the panic setting in to every fibre of his body as it fought valiantly to stay alive. His head remained lolled to one side, looking blankly at Stamford who remained talking senselessly.

His skin became paler with each passing second, growing clammy as his body tried to acclimatise to the sudden changes in temperature. Grain by grain the sands of his life ebbed away. Tears pooled in the corners of his eyes and slowly ran down his cheek.

Truman lay transfixed looking at Stamford with longing. For what – he did not know. He did not seek help from the man who had done this to him. Maybe it was a longing for release, for he was now a prisoner locked in his own fading body. His heart was slowing, running out of strength. His lungs had already given up unable to pull in any more oxygen.

Stamford's image became a blur. Not just because of the tears that now streamed from his eyes; his brain was starting to die. The absence of oxygen had found its way to the last vital organ that the poison had left to claim. The doctor's face faded into a pale cloud above a dark, shimmering trunk. The light around Stamford continued to shine, illuminating him as if he were an angel.

Stamford took a couple of steps toward the cot, his nose creasing up as he drew close to Truman. He had to mask his disgust at the smell of a body giving up, of organs failing, tissues dying and waste excreting. He slowly bent at the waist so that his mouth was next to Truman's ear. He needed to tell him one more thing before his mind was gone.

"They're coming."

Amidst everything around them that was beginning to fade, turn black and disappear, Truman saw the light that shone around Stamford, shadowing all of his other features.

The light continued to grow, taking over the room radiating searing warmth. The thrumming that Truman had heard since the needle went in grew louder until in manifested into vibrations that he could feel shaking the ground beneath him and the wall behind his head.

The rumbling became a scraping, followed by a clunk as stone met heavy stone. The colours began to return, rushing towards him as if pushed by a freight train, until suddenly his vision was clearer than before. The bright white light was still there and becoming brighter, absorbing all of the darkness from the cell and breathing it in. Truman turned his head, relieved he was able to move again.

Was he dead? Or was this the out-of-body experience that so many talked about, that came with the final rays of light?

It can't be, he decided as he moved his arm freely finding it did not leave behind the image of his limp, dead body underneath. He looked to the floor and found the source of the heavy thud that had woken him. Four feet away from his bed lay one of the stone blocks that made up the impenetrable wall of his cell. He looked towards the wall itself and saw a perfect aperture through which the light was burning through – not sunlight from the outside world but from the white light that he had already experienced before. The thud came again as another brick fell. Truman watched the wall torn away as if made of paper. The third stone flew towards them with a flash and Stamford disappeared from Truman's gaze, catapulted across to the opposite side where he lay slumped on the floor, his dazed limp body propped against the wall.

The stone had struck Stamford square in the chest, winding him and cracking his upper ribs. Truman remained on the bed, powerless to move, staring towards him, trying to make sense of what had happened – what was *still* happening around him. A faint moan escaped the doctor's lips, but there was no movement to suggest he was conscious.

Truman averted his gaze and fixated on the wall behind him. Brick by brick it was dismantling itself. The rest of the structure was falling outwards forming an unkempt pile of rubble. The light continued to glare brighter and brighter and Truman was forced to bring his hands up to shield his eyes. The heat was as unbearable as the brightness itself.

His hands…he could move them both up to his face with no effort. The shackles had fallen from his arms and even the cuff that belonged to the broken chain was gone – they had disappeared from sight.

"Ewan…Ewan…" the light sang, soothing him. Truman responded to his old name without trepidation. He looked up, straining his eyes, as a shadow drew closer to him from out of the white. He knew that voice and at that moment he knew that there was a chance for him. The light around the shadow faded enough for him to take in all of the heavenly features he hoped he would see.

"Evelyn," he rasped his throat dry. The heat and the poison had drained all moisture from him.

Evelyn appeared at the bedside, as present in the room as Stamford had been – no longer an illusion. Truman sat up on the cot, his legs hanging, his feet rested on the floor. There was no strength left his limbs. It did not matter though. At that moment he was safe.

"Ewan, we must leave," she said, "We must get away from here. They're coming."

"Who?"

"There's no time." The urgency was clear. She wanted to tell him everything but now was neither the time nor place. It was too dangerous for them both. "We must go," she reached for his hand.

"I must see them."

"No, Ewan! You can't. If they see you, I will lose you forever. There's too many of them."

His hand flinched. Her touch was cold. Not an unpleasant cold, a welcome one, a relief from the searing heat coming from the light that Evelyn brought with her. Evelyn calmly reached out and touched his hand again. This time he did not recoil or hesitate. He took her hand and rose to his feet. Although he knew his body was weak, it was not an effort supporting his own weight again. *How long had it been? Days, weeks, months?* He dare not speculate. As he stood, she led him away from the bed towards the now absent wall and into the bright light.

Truman paused looking back at the figure that lay against the wall. Stamford had started to stir. Truman stared at him wanting to know who he was, what he had done and why *any* of this was happening. He knew that he would not get the answers he craved – needed – from that man. Stamford looked back at him, his face more gaunt and tired than before.

"Ewan!" Evelyn tried to break Truman from his daze. "We have to go, they're too close…"

"I can't leave him,"

"You must! There's nothing you can do for him. He belongs to *them*."

As she spoke, Truman glanced over her shoulder and saw them. They started as spots, tiny black holes breaking through the walls of the white room that built itself around him. Then they grew. They grew outwards, upwards. They came together forming larger pools of nothingness. Just as he had witnessed before they began to grow and morph into beings of their own.

Unlike his vision, they were not hazy or made up of black smoke or shadows. They were foreign beings. Completely black, they appeared as solid entities with arms, legs, torsos and heads.

There were no faces.

The only feature that made the bulbous shape on top of their shoulders appear head-like were a set of burning red eyes. Truman stared unable to do anything more. He could not move. He barely even felt himself breathing. They continued to grow but in that instant he realised that they were not just growing; they were drawing closer, from a distance beyond the white light, being drawn towards it. Hundreds of sets of beastly red eyes shone towards him, never shifting and drawing nearer.

"We have to go!" Evelyn cried once more, above the thrumming that still pulsated through Truman. He thought it was the energy in the light that made the sound, like a million fireflies beating their wings in unison, but now it sounded like something more.

Something much worse.

Voices.

Hundreds of voices, speaking in another tongue, not of this world; chanting without lips. He listened for a few more seconds, trying to tune in to them and hear what they were saying. With the voices he began to react to energies running through his body again. The energy was telling him to move, to take Evelyn's hand and get as far away from the beings as possible. To stay would result in certain death. Not just the kind he had already witnessed but extinction; a failure to exist on any level in this world. He had never believed in a life after death but something had awoken in him.

He looked towards Evelyn whose eyes were pleading for him to take her hand and move with her once more. He took one more step and they headed towards the light. Stamford had just enough strength to push himself away from the cold stone wall. He fell towards Truman just as he was walking away. Then the light consumed Truman and the woman who had come for him.

Stamford lay alone on the floor of the cell now. As he pushed up on his arms to put himself in a sitting position, he looked around. Hundreds of red eyes looked back at him as the room became nothing more than a blanket of dark.

Stamford rested against the wall - the stone structure the only thing keeping his body upright as he gulped in fresh air, wanting to feel alive again. He had welcomed the light as soon as the cell door had burst open saving him from the darkness.

And those eyes. They had appeared to burn, trying to penetrate his mind, to tear away his skin. But he had been saved. That was all that mattered right now. He knew he could rely on Grayson. All of these years, the man had served him, protected him, and never judged. Now he had saved him from those *things* that wanted to devour his soul. The front courtyard of St. Dymphna's Research Facility situated in the most barren corner of Wildermoor at River's Peake, which had been his home for over twenty years, never looked so beautiful. Spring was on its way and soon it would be awash with bright colours and new promise.

He closed his eyes for a moment, his mind struggling to shut out the images and sounds of those moments he was alone in that room.

Those voices.

His breathing laboured again as he recalled the sound that grated his every nerve. They hissed, they growled, they moaned. They spat at him and he could feel their mouth-less faces breathing hot against his skin. The sound reverberated through him for what seemed like many painful hours – a cacophony of suffering. Eventually he felt he had become attuned to them and started making out words they were saying. His eyes remained tightly shut until one voice rose above the others in the darkness.

"Come…with…ussssss."

Stamford"s eyes popped open as the door creaked loudly, startling him, making his heart feel as though it had stopped dead. The sound had chased away the shadows and their voices. At the sight of Grayson's hulking form, shining like a beacon in the doorway, Stamford found the strength to jump to his feet despite his damaged ribs and run towards him. Whimpering, he was carried outside.

"How are you feeling now, sir?" The deep voice settled him instantly. "Here, take this," he handed Stamford a steaming polystyrene cup of coffee, fresh from the vending machine in the lobby. No-one besides Stamford had occupied the facility for years but he had insisted on keeping the coffee machine there.

"Thank you."

Grayson noticed the doctor was badly hurt and shaken up. He had no idea what had happened in the room and was afraid to ask. He was also concerned by Stamford's reaction when he enquired what had happened to his patient, the man they had taken from his temporary surgery room in Shepherd's Beach, the one that Stamford had obsessed over since he brought him back to the facility, and had devoted his life to since then.

It was as if he had just vanished. And whatever had happened must have been bad. It was the first time Stamford had refused to answer any of Grayson's questions or allay his concerns.

They stood in silence. Grayson watched Stamford take a few tentative sips of coffee, struggling to control the cup to his mouth for his shaking hands.

"So what happens now, boss?" Stamford stared across the horizon. Besides the imposing building behind them this side of Wildermoor was a vast nothingness. There were no prying residents, or lawmen had to watch out for or answer to.

Stamford knew his time was running out. He had failed, and whenever the images returned of Truman Darke/Ewan Childs walking away, disappearing into the burning light, clinically dead moments earlier, his insides dropped feeling as though they were detaching themselves from their warm casing and accepting the fate that awaited him. He had lost the one that held the key to the Council's sacred plan.

"It's over, Grayson. For me, at least."

The big man stared silently in disbelief at his employer. This man – the doctor – had displayed a passion so deep for his work that Grayson wondered if he had ever considered there was a life beyond it. Now virtually overnight, something had happened to make him give up.

Grayson hadn't noticed the black shape that appeared far on the horizon across Wildermoor hastily drawing closer. He watched Stamford as he stared coldly out across the plains - a man in the throes of submission.

Stamford finished his coffee with a loud gulp and without shifting his eyes, offered the empty cup back to Grayson.

"Please be a dear and take the rubbish inside and dispose of it. You know how I hate litter. Nothing should spoil this place."

Grayson took the cup and begrudgingly walked back through the lobby. Stamford knew that he had to walk to the very back of the building to find the only waste paper bin in the whole facility. He would be gone a while.

The doctor stood up straight, despite the pain from his chest causing him to wince, and raised his head high. Within moments, the black Mercedes turned into the gravel driveway leading to the courtyards. The driver, dressed head-to-toe in black, complete with black sunglasses, stepped out and opened the rear passenger door nearest to Stamford. Without a word exchanged between the two, just a nod on each part, Stamford stepped into the back seat of the car as the door closed brusquely behind him. Stamford exchanged a greeting with the man beside him. A stylish gentleman in a black suit, crisp white shirt and slick black hair looked vacantly towards him in a silent welcome.

"Your failure has caused great concern," the man said coldly as Stamford sank into the warm yet soulless, leather seat. "Your time is up, Mason."

By the time Grayson returned to the courtyard, Stamford and the Mercedes were nowhere to be seen.

Chapter Twenty-Nine

The sunlight sneaking in through the curtains was the only thing to wake Ewan, as he wrestled his eyes open turning onto his left side, he reached an arm out around Evelyn's body. Both were naked with only a thin sheet to protect them from the chill. He pulled her close, nuzzling against the back of her neck and kissed her. Both lay in silence.

It had been the same practice for three days. When Evelyn had saved him from the facility that night and led him into her light she had asked him where he wanted to go.

"Home," was his simple response. She knew that he did not mean his lonely one-bedroom flat in Bethesda Street. Home was Tewke's" Range. He remembered being appalled at the decrepit state the place had been left in. The later generations of the Childs" family not caring to maintain the majesty it once had. But those times were distant memories to Ewan; it felt as if he had never left the place.

That night, when he was led through the decaying front door, Ewan had collapsed and remained locked in a coma for two weeks. This time, the unconsciousness brought no images from the past or any pain. His body repaired itself steadily as he slept.

When he finally awoke, the house was alive again. The walls freshly painted, windows replaced and a new timber veranda erected at the rear of the building, adjoining the exit from the kitchen. The sight it provided was breathtaking – an unspoilt view across Wildermoor taking in the vast plains as they rolled to the bordering forests. The range's land lay void of crops but Ewan decided he would change that. He and Evelyn finally had the home that he had longed for.

That night at the facility was still a blur, as was the life he left behind in that room. He was home, in body and spirit, and that was all that mattered. Evelyn had done her best to fill Ewan in on the events that had brought them back together, but she had been instructed to spoon-feed him information as he regained his strength. He deserved to know everything, but his mind was still recovering. It would all be too much.

His body healed nicely. The bathing light that Evelyn had brought forth had evaporated the poison that had shut his body down and allowed Ewan to leave with her that night. The rest was up to him. He had to build his mental strength before she could lead him any further down the rabbit hole.

However, this day everything felt different. They had woken and lain together in silence. The silence lasting for one hour then two. Then a third, until the morning had passed with no words. They had spent the time in each other's arms. Ewan thankful for each minute that he had with Evelyn, but trying not to admit something was wrong. Something was hanging over the both of them, something he could not explain.

"You've still not told me why you came back for me," Ewan said cautiously as they both sat on the bank. He cradled her from behind in a reverse bear hug. He had asked the question many times but she had always changed the subject. That day something felt different. Evelyn knew that she could not avoid it forever. She continued to gaze out across Wildermoor, admiring the beautiful scarred surface that proved the moor had fought against everything nature had thrown at her. Ewan craned his neck to see her face, to check that she was still with him.

"An end is coming," she said still staring ahead, "the likes of which have never been witnessed."

Her soft voice contrasted the words it released. An air of finality lingered for a few moments as Ewan tried to make sense of it.

"An end to what?"

"This…" she replied sweeping her head in an arc to signify the land before them. Ewan followed her action, but failed to follow what she was saying.

"This? You mean Wildermoor?"

"It starts here."

Ewan tightened his grip around Evelyn's waist, worried that she was suffering from a fever, which was affecting her thoughts.

"I don't understand," It was the truth if not an understatement. She was definitely making him feel uneasy and he had no idea what to do.

Evelyn finally turned her head to the side and their eyes locked. Tears were starting to well, giving her piercing blue eyes a depth that concerned him. If he stared into them for too long, he himself would be lost. There was something happening – something big – that she was keeping from him and struggling to tell him.

"The Council – the same who were in the caves the night that I was there when they took my father's life - that very evil still hangs over this place. It is nearing the time that it will claim this land for its own. They still reside here in Wildermoor. They have remained hidden for over three hundred years lying in wait for Him to return."

Her voice was starting to tremble as she spoke, having the same effect on Ewan's hands. He felt such an overwhelming fear, and willed it to stop. But it was no use. He wanted to believe that her ramblings were just that, but something in her eyes told him otherwise.

"And now He has, they are readying their troops. As must we."

"We? Evelyn, what are you saying? You're making no sense. Who is *we*? And what is this *end*? You're tired, we both are. Too much has happened in the last couple of weeks for either of us to -"

"Don't you get it?" She snapped cutting him off, breaking free from his warm grip, finding her feet. "In a matter of months – maybe even weeks – none of this will exist!"

"I am trying to understand, Evelyn, I really am! But I barely know who I am anymore, where I am, if any of this is even real. Now you're talking as if the world is going to end and there's no hope for…I don't know, all of this is just a little hard to take in right now."

She stepped forward to meet him once more and locked her lips to his. They both lingered for a few moments lost in each other. When they fell apart again, Evelyn looked up through her tears.

"Now tell me I'm not real." Ewan was reaching his own breaking point and turned his back not wanting her to see him crack. He was losing the strength he needed to protect them both.

"I know this is hard for you, Ewan, and I don't even know where to start with all of this. But are you telling me that you can make sense of *anything* that has happened to you recently? Why is this any different?"

His mind returned to the vision that he had back in the cell, as he looked across the plains of Wildermoor burning as if lit by the flames of the sun, the shadows advancing, those eyes, the screaming voices and the hooded figure that stood between them all.

Ewan's mind fired images behind his eyes, bringing back images from a past that he had started to leave behind, one he left behind centuries ago but that swamped him again. His mind flickered back to the day he had returned from his coma, the day that he woke up and found himself back at Tewke's Range. Evelyn had only broken one bit of news to Ewan that day. She presented him with a copy of the day's Wildermoor Herald. The headline read:

MORE MISSING. POLICE CHIEF PLAYS DOWN RECENT RISE IN DISAPPEARANCES.

Ewan did not notice the photo of the well-groomed DI Thomas Laing next to the headline.

The date - March *26th, 2012.*

Ten years lost as though they never existed at all.

He dropped the paper onto the kitchen table, overcome by a wave of disorientation and nausea, and returned to bed unable to face the rest of the day. There had been no mention of it when he re-surfaced and Evelyn had not dared to bring it up again. They had lived for some time happy in their own bubble.

"This can't be happening," his voice was breaking as he stared back towards Tewke's Range.

"Ewan..." Evelyn tenderly reached for his shoulder. He flinched and shrugged her off. He wanted to lash out, push her away and tell her she was wrong. But he couldn't. He wanted to keep her close to him in case she was cruelly snatched away from him again and apart from a few scattered memories and haunting visions, he knew nothing of the life he had woken up with.

Everything had changed. Was he expected to accept that?

"What do I do?" He turned away from her. He couldn't bear to see what was behind her eyes or show her his. "What part do I play in all of this?"

"Follow me," she replied, "I will show you."

She led him back into the house, letting him catch up to her and allowing his hand to link into hers. Inside, she fished out a leather satchel she had left in the old store room. Returning to the kitchen, she laid the bag on the table and withdrew a package from inside. She handed a plain brown, padded envelope to Ewan and he closed his hand around it.

"This will tell you everything you need to know but I have one request."

He returned her gaze with a raised eyebrow urging her to continue.

"Open it when I've gone."

His face darkened unable to hide the hurt that she sent surging through him.

"You're not staying with me?"

His eyes resembled that of a child being left behind by their parent with no explanation as to why.

She shook her head and released a tear that she had valiantly held. Her voice shook as she tried to speak, taking a couple of attempts to compose herself for what she knew she had to do.

"I do not belong here anymore; I have a new home now." She saw the defiance in his eyes as he shook his head, not wanting to listen. She gently grabbed him by the arm to stop him from turning away. "But neither do you. Just as I had a task to complete, you too have yours."

Ewan looked at more confused than before. His head was spinning out of control and he had the urge to run out of the door into the wilderness and never look back. But he forced himself to hear her out. If she was going to hurt him, break his heart and take away all of his hope, he was sure she must have a good reason. He wanted to hear it for himself.

"That night in the caves, I felt no pain. As soon as my body was killed, my spirit was saved. There is an existence beyond here – beyond this realm – referred to as the Trinity. Three of the highest powers in existence help save those of us who have been wronged in life, lives brought to an end too soon, destined for better things. You have to be chosen and that night I was."

She saw by his glazed expression that she was losing Ewan. He was losing himself to anger and loss. She needed to keep him with her or risk losing him forever.

"A war is coming, one that will be fought between the shadows and the light. It will soon invade the reality that we both know. They have found a way to breach the boundaries, between their world, my world and yours. As their Leader gains strength, it is becoming easier for them to invade this land taking whomever they want." Her voice was grave as her gaze fell to the floor.

"This is makes no sense," said Ewan fighting his instinct to put his hands over his ears and ignore anything else that was happening.

"Those who are chosen are given a chance to move towards divinity, to an eternal life beyond death. It is done in three stages – they are called Elevations. Only when you achieve the Third Elevation are you truly saved; until then we remain prey for the shadows. The First Elevation is the act of being chosen, being saved after your body has died and being given a chance. A mission – assignment – must be completed before each Elevation. Each assignment requires a soul to be saved. This," she motioned towards the envelope he had tightly in his hand, "is your assignment. Only you can complete it and only you can save this person."

Ewan stared at the envelope as if he was searching for the answers written in invisible ink on the outside.

"Where do you fit in all of this?"

"I have achieved my Second Elevation. You were the soul I needed to save."

A painful silence hung between them.

"So what now?"

"I have a job to do and now," she moved closer to him, stroking the sides of his floppy hair back behind his ears, "so do you."

He looked down at the envelope, and then back to her. Both their faces were streaked with tears.

"We will have our time," she reassured him, "but not here, not now."

"Why me?" He asked the burning question that had built over years.

She sighed hoping to avoid telling him more than she had already, knowing his full purpose would be too much pressure. *Spare him that weight.*

She looked at him aware the child within had become frail and weak once more. She could not send him into this without being fully prepared.

"You're the most important link to all of this, which is why I have been given so many years to complete my assignment. The Reaper is looking for you, as he knows this too. You're the last link to his bloodline, something he needs to absorb in order to make his transformation complete and bring all of this to an end."

Ewan stood silently for a moment before it all came flooding back to him. That night in the woods, the fire, the screaming and the pain that Katrina endured for years.

"Lucas…" he whispered. Evelyn nodded. "You said bloodline but that's impossible. I took him in as a brother but we were not bound by blood. He had no family."

He could hear words echo around the cold kitchen although they existed only in his head. The night he had hidden in the trees and witnessed Stamwell's murder;

"Your son Stamwell, for my brother. If you will not give your life for his."

"Oh my God," Ewan muttered the words staring at the floor. "All this time…?"

"Time matters no more, my love, "Evelyn soothed trying to bring Ewan back once more, "Time will cease to exist if we cannot do this."

Ewan turned from her again, trying to steady his breath and reclaim the thoughts as his own. In life he had not considered he amounted to anything and now he was here with the fate and weight of the world resting on his shoulders. There was no escape, He knew that. If he wanted the chance to live again, to live that life with Evelyn, this was what he had to do.

The Reaper.

The phantom he had dispelled as nothing more than ravings of a madman. *Colin Dexler.* Slowly it all began to make sense.

"Evelyn, I never got to say it before, and may not have the chance to say it again so it's now or never. I…" he turned around to find he was alone in the kitchen. "…love you."

He ran out of the door and was greeted by the rolling, empty lands of Wildermoor. It was a sight that he both loved and loathed. This was the place that gave birth to him, killed him and shackled him to it forever. Still it asked for more. He nodded a grim acceptance still not fully understanding but knowing that he wanted to.

He looked down at the envelope that was still grasped in his hand, starting to crease and bend as his fists clenched. He tore open the seal and removed the contents: a thick document of around a hundred pages, containing separate files and photos clipped to the sheets haphazardly throughout. As the envelope tipped in his hand, another object slipped out and fell to the ground; a leather wallet. Ewan picked it up and turned it over finding a bright yellow post-it note on the other side.

We are who we are but don't forget all you have been. I love you too. I will be waiting. Evelyn.

The wallet opened like a book - no clasp to hold it shut – and the gold badge glimmered as the sun emerged behind a heavy cloud ahead. Ewan smiled humourlessly to himself as he stared at the name written on the other side. A shiver ran down the length of his back as heavy storm clouds returned and reclaimed the sun. He turned back towards the house as the shadows grew and he felt the eyes on his back. Not hundreds this time, just one set. The heat behind him grew as fierce as it did in his vision of the burning moors.

Ewan looked behind to find nothing had changed, but he could feel Him watching.

Waiting.

If you enjoyed *Acolyte*, you'll love

The Sowing Season

The next gripping instalment of the Wilmoor Apocalypse trilogy.

March 1684

After witnessing her lover's brutal ritualistic murder, Katrina Childs returns home a shell of her former self. Her only hope is of the child growing inside of her.

A mysterious old man appears in the village one night with a warning for her brother, Ewan: Protect Katrina and her child at all costs.

Lucas Stamwell will return to claim them both.

March 2012

Jacob Crowe is living a simple life, surrounded by the tranquillity and protection that only Wildermoor can bring. Until the night that his wife is torn away from him by dark spirits, as he is stalked by a hooded phantom.

Jacob is saved from The Reaper's clutches by Truman Darke, who has returned to Wildermoor ten years after he was abducted by The Council of Eternal Light. The Council's plans for a new world enter the next terrifying phase as The Reaper grows his demon army, by setting his umbras free to claim souls to add to their ranks...and feast on those that are left.A process that He refers to as 'The Sowing Season'.

DI Thomas Laing is forced to aid their case, having had to choose between his family and his future.

December 2012

As the planned apocalypse rapidly approaches, the Council's own security is compromised by a rookie journalist interested in the whereabouts—and importance—of the mysterious Patient 29; a man said to be housed within the walls of St. Dymphna's Research Facility.

To find the answers to save their future, they must all look to their past.

Read on for an extract of the book here...

Chapter One

Woodlands, three miles south of Devil's Pit

The lightning provided the only clues to the pathway as it lit the sky above, squeezing through the tops of the trees as Ewan's arms finally grew tired. His legs were not letting him down though and they marched on, carrying the burden. He was sure that they were now far enough away that the hooded men would not be following them. Ewan looked down at the fragile young woman in his arms; his sister Katrina. Her body had finally succumbed to sleep. Ewan could not bear to look into her eyes any more that night and see the pain rooted so deeply in them, so he was glad that she was no longer awake. The silence, however, did nothing but whisper blame to him.

He had been too late. For both of them.

He arrived only just in time to see Stamwell's body burning, tied helplessly to his own crucifixion post. His eyes only saw Katrina as she scrambled to her feet and ran into the cover of the trees. Ewan ran after her for what seemed like miles before he realised that he had somehow cut across her path and was in fact in front of her. As he began to gingerly double-back on his tracks, forever conscious of the demonic gathering that had witnessed – caused – his friend's death, he soon found her.

His heart ached as he saw her on her knees, her dress torn and covered in mud to the waist, her body arched as it struggled for breath through her sobs.

For a moment, Ewan hated Stamwell for what he had done to her. He had come into her life, stolen her heart and then had selfishly given himself up to a torturous end, forcing Katrina to watch. But it quickly occurred to Ewan that Stamwell could not have been blamed for his own death; he had given his own life to spare Katrina's. Ewan also realised that it had been he who had brought Stamwell back to Tewke's Range with him, into his sister's life.

He ran the last few yards to gather Katrina into his arms and was surprised when she suddenly stood steady on her feet and angrily beat at his chest. Through her cries, he knew she was blaming him too, asking him why he had not been there to save the man she loved.

Ewan could say nothing, for he knew she was right. He could have – should have – done more, even just to have been there a few minutes earlier. But could he have really spared Stamwell's life from the mob that had so cruelly put him to the flame? He guessed not, for he had also witnessed the extent of their power the night Stamwell helped him escape the caves. But it was no use, for he knew that no justification that he could give to what had happened that night to Stamwell could ever bring him back, therefore would never alter the fact that his own sister would no longer look to her brother as a hero.

Ewan eventually allowed himself a break to recharge his aching limbs, laying Katrina onto a soft bed of leaves by the riverside. He smiled to himself briefly as he realised that he was back at the same spot that he had camped on the final night of his search for his own lost love, Evelyn James. That night had ended badly, resulting in him finding a few remnants of the men who rode with him, and started the disastrous journey back with the girl's father to find her a few nights later.

That night he lost his own father too, and he would be damned if he would let the same people take away his sister. How much of her would remain after that night, he would never know.

Ewan drank from the river and after a while felt fit to press on again, so lifted Katrina back into his arms and carried on. She had not awoken, had not stirred in the slightest. The gentle rising of her chest was the only clue that she was still with him in some way. Ewan wrapped his coat around her, adding to the weight he was now carrying, and allowed his mind to go blank; unaware of the pain setting in to his legs and dispelling the horrific visions that still replayed behind his eyes. It was all coming back to him in lightning-speed fashion; the night in the caves, the monster that he had watched tear bodies to shreds as if made from paper, to the apparition of his sister that visited him in the darkness of the Weary Traveller's cellar, and finally the smells and sounds of watching another man cooked at the stake. He, as much as his sister, needed to think of nothing at all if he was going to make it back to Tewke's Range without losing any more time. Or indeed his own mind. Almost two hours later, with the moon full and heavy in the sky, they returned home.

Ewan walked straight up the stairs and laid Katrina down onto the neatly-made bed, which she had lovingly made only that morning. That morning she had awoken with a man beside her who made her feel safe. Tomorrow she would awaken cold, broken and alone. Ewan knew that he had to be there for her when she woke up, to shoulder all of her pain and try his best to rebuild her. But morning was still hours away. What he needed right then, more than anything, was a drink.

Satisfied that Katrina was finally safe, he locked the door and left the lifeless home behind him as he walked down to The Weary Traveller.

*****

The Traveller was bustling with activity, a hazy veil of smoke hanging above all of the tables as the regular patrons puffed away on cigars whilst enjoying another full pint of the finest ales their side of England. A few raised their heads and nodded greetings as they saw Ewan, the pub's landlord, enter. He returned a few himself, with a painted smile as he walked to the bar. Florence, the only barmaid that the inn had known for almost twenty years, crossed behind the bar to where he stood as soon as she saw him. As she approached, the smile slowly fell from her face, replaced with a wide stare.

"What the hell's happened, duck? You bolted form here like a bullet from a gun. Are you okay? Is anything wrong?"

Ewan had grown up around Florence and was used to her motherly ways, always concerned for him and his brothers, making something out of nothing mostly. As well as being a mother-figure to him, she had also been the object of his affections during his most hormonally-challenging years. Her face was still as smooth as he imagined it had been when she had been in her teens, her dress straining to hold back the form that god had given her; all in the right places, of course. He had always felt that he could tell her anything but as he went to speak now, the words never came. Ewan couldn't even bring himself to tell of everything that had happened in the last few hours, he didn't know how or where to start. He just placed his hand on hers on top of the bar, forced a smile and told her that it was nothing that couldn't be fixed with a drink. Without any further prompting, she poured him a measure from a bottle of the top-shelf whiskey. He downed it and offered the glass back to her. He was thankful when she was called to serve another thirsty customer, as he could resist those eyes no longer. They were pools of blue that he knew many men could – and probably had – gotten themselves lost in during many a cosy night in front of the open fire at the Traveller. His father had often joked that she was the reason why their takings were so good and was the only reason he had kept her on for so long. The truth was, Ewan knew, that there had been more between Florence and his father than just chit-chat behind the bar.

Ewan looked back over his shoulder and scanned the activity across the pub. Everything was as it always had been. It was as if he had crossed some inter-dimensional plane that night when he had entered the woods, where only fear and terror guided him and his most stomach-churning nightmares awaited him at the end. Everyone seemed oblivious of the dangers that existed around their sleepy little village, and Ewan found himself comforted by that fact.

His eyes met an unnerving stare, however, from a face he had never seen before. Having spent much of his child- and man-hood in the Traveller, he knew almost every face that called in at any time, day or night. But this man was new to him, and the way he looked at him put him on edge, just at the moment that he had finally started to feel relaxed. This man, whoever he was, immediately brought back all of the visions that had haunted him during the long journey back from Devil's Pit. Ewan turned away, shouted towards Florence and asked for another drink.

As she walked back to him, Ewan leant in and whispered to her. "Who's the guy in the corner, on his own?" He signalled with a nod behind him. Florence flashed her eyes in the intended direction and lowered them back to Ewan. 'I don't know. He has been in here for three nights running now. He hardly speaks except when ordering a pint.' Ewan saw that she was thinking as she spoke, as if she had more to tell him but was struggling to find the best way to approach it.

"He's been asking about you. Where you were, when you'd be back. In face he only arrived here tonight ten minutes before you did, but asked the same question as he ordered his drink. Very odd, but he seems to be keeping himself to himself the rest of the time."

Ewan pondered her words for a moment, trying to decide whether the man sounded like a threat or a friend. It was not unknown for businessmen to arrive in town wanting to speak to the proprietor of the successful village drinking hole, and Ewan's father had been offered and tempted more than once by lucrative offers from outsiders.

"I tell you what, Flo; I may as well make myself useful. I will gather some glasses back for you."

She smiled and nodded eagerly, pleased that he seemed more like his old self. Work was obviously something that could help ease his mind, whatever was troubling him. If that didn't help, she thought, maybe she could find another way to help him after closing. She watched as he crossed between the tables, exchanging quiet yet jolly conversation with each of the punters that looked up from their beers long enough to speak to him. Then she saw him approach the outsider's table and nervously averted her gaze, finding an excuse to turn her back to check the supplies behind her. Despite having her back turned, she kept one ear open to try and listen above the din of the raucous crowd.

Ewan watched the man as he drew closer to his table, the stranger's own eyes widening as he watched him.

"Can I get you another?" Ewan offered.

"Please, yes, same again. Thank you." His tone was gruff but warming. Ewan found that he was even more confused, unable to figure him out as he was hoping he would by his vocal delivery. Ewan returned behind the bar and poured the man's drink himself and took it over to him. As he placed the dripping tankard on the table, the man spoke again.

"You're Ewan Childs, aren't ya?"

Ewan looked blankly at the man for a moment, focusing on his eyes. They shone a peculiar colour; one that Ewan had not seen before. Sapphire orbs like beacons, drawing Ewan unwittingly to the man. The light in the room appeared to flicker and dampen, then just as quickly grow again as he found himself back in some form of reality.

"Who wants to know?"

"Yeah you're him alright," the man smiled.

"What's it to you?" Ewan asked cagily.

"Take a seat, let me speak with you," the stranger said, making room on the padded bench for him.

"I'm sorry, I'm working. It's a busy night and I'm afraid I can't just drop everything to speak with a-"

"I've been sent with a warning, son." The strangely-coloured eyes suddenly grew brighter, making Ewan shudder as a chill blew across his back. "You may want to hear me out."

Ewan let a single laugh escape before gathering his reply. "A warning? For me? I don't take warnings from anyone," he leaned in closer to speak to the man in a whisper. "Especially someone who thinks they are above giving me their name…*sir*." He spat the last word at the man and surprised himself how harsh he could sound. The night had already changed him and he wasn't sure whether he was going to like how.

"Forgive me. The name's Elijah. Elijah Strong." He held out a friendly hand and Ewan faltered for a moment as he looked into his face. He sure did not look familiar – the square jaw, the head of white hair cut close to the scalp, the chin coated in light grey stubble. Ironically, he could have been any of the landowners across Wildermoor, with a face which told a story of a lifetime of toil and hands that were scarred by hard work. Harsh but handsome, that's how his mother would have described him. Yes, Ewan thought, this man could surely win the ladies over with a look or two. But it was those eyes that drew him in.

"I'm sorry, Mr. Strong. I didn't mean to sound off-hand. It has been a long day and unfortunately I feel that I have neglected my duties here today. Maybe we can arrange another time, for tonight I really must get on."

As Ewan turned to leave, Elijah shouted loud enough for Ewan to hear him but not loud enough to travel to any of the eager ears around them. "It's about your sister, Mr. Childs."

Ewan stopped dead in his tracks and slowly turned around, his face scowled. He took two steps back to Elijah's table. "You have my attention and about one minute of my time before I personally escort you from my premises." Elijah nodded silently, extending a hand towards the empty seat next to him. Ewan decline once again.

"More to the point, it's about the child." Elijah could tell by Ewan's face that he still did not understand; he must have had no idea that she was carrying life within her belly. "Yes, she is with child. Sired by a man she loved but a man that, unfortunately, already had another life waiting for him. You cannot be mad at him however, Mr. Childs, for he had no idea. And he is no longer with us. But he will return soon, firstly for your sister and then for their child."

As he let Elijah speak, the strength started to seep from Ewan's legs and he found that he needed the offer of a seat after all, and sat next to him as he listened. His mouth and eyes opened wide, telling the old man that he was indeed listening. Not only listening, but believing. As much as the Ewan did not want to face up to what he was telling him, Elijah knew that he would accept it all as fact. He had no choice.

"You must protect them both, Mr. Childs. At all costs."

Ewan tried to speak but his throat and mouth were raw and no sound came. Strong offered him some of his beer, which he gratefully accepted. After gulping down the sweet amber, Ewan was ready to speak. "But how? Lucas is dead. I saw it with my own eyes. No man could survive that kind of fate."

"The men who took his life have also given him a new existence, one that I fear not even they can control. To begin with, he will be driven by the most basic of human emotions; love and hate. The love he will still hold for your sister will soon fade, but the love for their child will grow as it too grows inside her. I must warn you, Mr. Childs, that if he gets his hand on the child, the love he harbours will steadily turn to hate for everything left around him. A hate that these men will aim to use against us all."

Ewan sat dumbfounded, in need of another drink of his own. "Please excuse me for a moment." He stood and his jellied legs guided him to the bar once again, but as he turned to walk back to the table, Elijah Strong was gone. Only his half-finished beer remained on the table, with a scrawled note underneath the glass.

"*You must find a way. When the time is right, I will return.*"

Ewan's whole body felt numb as he slumped into the seat that had been occupied by the man that had just turned his world upside-down. His brain fuzzed with everything that he had just heard, unable to digest it as fact or fiction. He looked again at the night and folded it and shoved it into his pocket, downing his own beer in only a few strikes. His head now hazed and his gait staggering, Ewan made his way back home. Florence stood watching him silently from the doorway leading to the cellar, her heart suddenly heavy for him.

www.ingramcontent.com/pod-product-compliance
Lightning Source LLC
Chambersburg PA
CDIIW030913060726
47591CB00005B/1521